"Are you okay?"

The solid but quiet voice of her rescuer was familiar, and not just from tonight. Claire's eyes narrowed as she looked up at him. "I know you," she said, studying his face as she took a step closer to him. "Where do I know you from?"

He studied her in return. "I recognized you right away, but then again you've changed less since college than I have."

"College..." she mumbled.

As though she'd summoned the memories up, a collage of snapshots from her college life played through her mind...including the man she now recognized as the one standing in front of her. Nate Torres.

Nate was the epitome of everything she'd never fall for again. But while he was the last man on earth she'd get involved with, he *was* someone she trusted.

Claire swallowed hard. "Nate Torres. Do you want to tell me what you're doing in Treasure Point? It's too much of a coincidence that someone tried to kill me and that you just happened to be in the right position to save me. There's something more going on here, isn't there?"

For a minute he didn't say anything, just stood there. Still and speechless.

Then he spoke. "Yes."

Sarah Varland lives near the mountains in Alaska, where she loves writing, hiking, kayaking and spending time with her family. She's happily married to her college sweetheart, John, and is the mom of two active and adorable boys, Joshua and Timothy, as well as another baby in heaven. Sarah has been writing almost since she could hold a pencil and especially loves writing romantic suspense, where she gets to combine her love for happily-ever-afters, inspired by her own, with her love for suspense, inspired by her dad, who has spent a career in law enforcement. You can find Sarah online through her blog, espressoinalatteworld.blogspot.com.

Books by Sarah Varland

Love Inspired Suspense

Treasure Point Secrets
Tundra Threat
Cold Case Witness
Silent Night Shadows

Visit the Author Profile page at Harlequin.com.

Silent Night Shadows

Sarah Varland

 HARLEQUIN® LOVE INSPIRED® SUSPENSE

Recycling programs
for this product may
not exist in your area.

LOVE INSPIRED BOOKS

ISBN-13: 978-0-373-44781-7

Silent Night Shadows

Copyright © 2016 by Sarah Varland

www.Harlequin.com

Printed in U.S.A.

But the Lord said to Samuel, "Do not look on his appearance or on the height of his stature, because I have rejected him. For the Lord sees not as man sees: man looks on the outward appearance, but the Lord looks on the heart."

–1 Samuel 16:7

To law enforcement officers—past and present—
who make sacrifices no one sees. Thank you for what you do.

Acknowledgments

Once again, I need to thank my family. Every day with you is
a gift, and I am so thankful to have you to love, and thankful
for your love for me. Thanks for letting me sit on the living
room floor, staring at the mountains out of the back window
now and then while I try to sort a story out in my mind.

Thanks to my writing friends. I always want to list you,
and then I get worried I will miss someone. But
you know who you are and I am deeply grateful for you.

I also appreciate my agent, Sarah, as well as my editor
Elizabeth and the behind-the-scenes people who worked on
the book, as well. Every book is an effort made by
so many more people than just the author, and
I am thankful to get to be part of the team at Harlequin.

Many thanks again to God, Who always teaches me something
through the stories I write, even when I am stubborn and
don't want to learn. Thank You for Your never-giving-up love.

ONE

The cool, dark December night wrapped around Claire Phillips, making her shiver deep inside. She wrapped her arms tighter around herself, wishing she'd grabbed her jacket before she'd left the coffee shop to head toward the town square for the tree lighting ceremony. But there hadn't been time. She'd promised her sister she'd meet her there at six, and it was already five till.

Claire glanced to her right and left. No one was around. Everyone seemed to be at the square already, and Claire rubbed at goose bumps that weren't just from the cold. She'd walked this route by herself more times than she could count, but right now she felt off somehow. Claire could feel a certain tension in the air, like tonight was a rubber band, stretched back.

And something was about to break.

Lately she'd felt watched. Not all the time, but sometimes when she was walking around town, she'd felt like someone was tracking her movements. She'd been debating with herself all day whether or not she should say something to her sister—Gemma's husband was a police officer and would know if she needed to report that or anything. Claire was leaning towards yes now, she decided. She hurried her steps a little, glancing behind her even as she told herself she was overreacting. She didn't see anything in the orange glow of the streetlights, or even beyond them in the darkness. None of the shadows that were familiar to her after a lifetime of living in this town seemed remotely out of place. So why couldn't she relax?

The noise from the crowd at the square grew louder. Claire could see the tree now, still dark, but about to be illuminated with brilliant colored lights. She allowed herself a small smile as she slowed her pace slightly to enjoy the moment. She was close now, close enough to let her guard down just a bit, admit that she'd been overreacting...

The rough hands that grabbed her from behind and pulled her into a row of shrubs just at the back of the square were fast, too fast for her to react once she was firmly in their grip.

The Treasure Point High School band started to play "O Christmas Tree." Loudly. Any attempt at a scream would go unheard, even this close to the crowds. Perfect timing on the part of whoever had her, Claire realized with clarity. Someone who knew the town and its traditions?

She tried to scream anyway but recoiled immediately at the sweaty, damp palm that was clapped over her mouth as soon as she did so. Now only one of the hands was holding her back by her arm, so she fought, struggled, tried to get away. Even after she used her shoulders to try to break free and elbowed behind her several times, connecting with some part of him, she was no closer to free than she'd been before exhausting herself. Her abductor was too strong.

Abductor. Her mind started to go hazy. What was going on? What was happening?

She heard approaching footsteps. Heavy ones like they belonged to a man—and no small man, either. She tensed, afraid to hope that it was someone to help her.

God, please.

It was all she could pray, but her faith meant too much to her not to attempt to trust her God, even in this.

"Let her go."

The voice was familiar to her. She was sure that the man was someone she'd seen recently, but not someone she knew well... Claire couldn't see behind her, but when the hands holding her didn't release her, she heard the solid connection of a punch. From the way the body behind her rocked with the blow, she assumed the punch came from her rescuer, whoever he was. Her abductor was holding her with just one hand now, using the other to defend himself. She braced herself as the fight continued. Not long after, her attacker ran toward the dock.

Claire was free.

Her rescuer followed for a few seconds, but then stopped and turned back to check on her. In the glow of the streetlight, she could see him clearly. For the first time, Claire looked at the man who'd saved her. The first thing she noticed was his black leather jacket. The second was his equally dark eyes that were looking at her without flinching.

Something about those eyes was familiar. She'd just felt her own eyes narrow as her study of him deepened when he looked away, broke the contact.

"Thank you," she finally said, her voice shaking more than she would have liked.

"Listen to me." He ignored the thanks, kept talking

in a voice that was 100 percent steady and gave no hint of being out of breath, even after that altercation.

"Go inside that store." He motioned to the nearest shop that hadn't closed for the night, Marsh Maze Books. "Call the police. Stay there until they come."

Before Claire could speak, the man took off running in the direction of the docks. Going after her attacker? Head spinning, she did what he'd told her to and walked straight into the shop.

"Bree! I didn't know you were working tonight."

Her friend looked up from the papers she'd been shuffling through at the counter and smiled. "Hey Claire!" Her smile fell a little. "You don't look so great. What's up?"

"I need to call the police, and I needed to be somewhere safe."

Her eyes widened. "Do you need to use the phone?"

Claire shook her head. "I've got mine. But thanks." She could see the questions in her friend's eyes, but she was unable to find words to explain anything and didn't want to have to tell the story twice. So instead of explaining, Claire listened to the phone ring until the operator picked up.

"This is Claire Phillips. I'm at Marsh Maze Books right now, but I was just attacked on my way to the square."

The operator's reassuring voice asked for more information, and Claire told her what she could, then hung up the phone.

Bree was still staring at her.

"I don't want to talk about it yet," she told her friend as she kept her eyes focused on the door, trying to figure out anything she could do to help her stay calm until officers arrived at the scene.

"O-okay," Bree stammered. "But…can I get you anything? Some water, maybe? Or do you want to sit down?"

"No water, thanks," Claire managed to say, though she did take the offer to have a seat on one of the overstuffed easy chairs scattered throughout the store. The adrenaline rush from earlier was fading, leaving her feeling more than a little unsteady on her feet.

Funny, maybe it was just the aftermath of the attack, some rush of numbness that had hit her, but when the Man in Black—as she'd started thinking of him—had rescued her, she'd felt oddly calm with him. Like his very presence affected her somehow. That was strange since, though Claire thought she'd seen him in her shop often in the past week or so, he was a stranger to her.

Why had he told her to call the police and then run? Her mind could take that question in so many different directions. Had he known the person who attacked her? Was he working with him somehow? But that didn't make sense. Then again, nothing did so far. Why would anyone want to hurt her? She ran a coffee shop in Treasure Point. As far as she knew, she didn't have any enemies at all. Yes, there had been some scary moments for Gemma earlier in the year, but everything had been worked out. Life should have been safe again.

It unsettled her, somewhere very close to her core, to know that apparently, life wasn't safe for her. Not right now.

Claire hugged her arms tight around herself and hunched deeper into the chair. To her credit, Bree didn't push for an explanation anymore, just stood there silently, not sure what to do. And Claire didn't blame for her for that—she didn't know what to do, either.

From far away across the square, Claire could see the tree lighting up slowly, from the bottom to the very top. It was a Treasure Point tradition, one she'd participated in every year—even the ones when she'd been on holiday break from college—with her parents and sister. This year her parents were on an extended vacation in New England, visiting some of her mom's relatives for the holidays, but Gemma was at the ceremony and Claire had planned to meet her.

Gemma. How could she not have texted her sister by now? Claire pulled her phone out.

I can't make it.

She could think of nothing else to say, so she just sent it.

Gemma's reply appeared seconds later.

What's up? Are you okay?

Claire messaged back,

Long story. Call me on your way home?

Okay.

A squad car pulled up just as she read Gemma's last text. Claire slid the phone into her pocket.

"Are you okay, Claire?"

Her brother-in-law was the first one in the door, followed by his friend Clay, another officer. Claire got to her feet. "Matt! I thought you were with Gemma?"

He shook his head. "I got called in at the last minute. Someone else had to go home sick. Tell us what happened."

"Right here? Or at the police station, or—?"

"Start with telling us where the attack happened."

"It was outside, down the street a little more toward my shop. I was walking toward the square when a man grabbed me, pulled me off the street."

"Did you see his face?" Clay asked.

Claire shook her head. "He held me from behind. I couldn't see him at all. But he was tall. Strong."

"Did you hear his voice?" Matt prompted. "Did he say anything?"

"He didn't, no. But then another man came up and said to let me go. He started fighting the man holding me, got him to release me and then run off."

"How did you end up in here?"

"The guy who helped me told me to come in here and call the police."

The two officers glanced at each other. Claire wished she could read the look that passed between them.

"Let's go on down to the station," Matt said. "Hitchcock, you go check out the street, make sure you don't see any evidence, though I doubt the attacker left any."

Clay nodded and headed out the door.

"Come on. The chief is going to want to hear this firsthand." Claire said goodbye to Bree, thanked her for her help, and then followed Matt through the doorway, grateful that if she had to go to the police station, at least she was close to the officer who was taking her in. She tried so hard always to seem put together, in control. Right now, she felt like she was falling apart. The officers of the Treasure Point police station were good people, most of whom she'd known for years, but there weren't many whom she'd want to see her like this.

Matt opened the passenger door for her, and she climbed in. She couldn't help but look around once she was sitting safely in the car, looking for any sign either of the man who'd attacked her or of the man who'd likely saved her life.

Nate's search of the docks had turned up nothing. Jesse Carson had gotten away.

Claire had shown no signs of recognizing her attacker, but Nate did. He was heading an investigation for the Georgia Bureau of Investigation that had been tracking the Carson brothers for the last eighteen months, trying to find out where they got their supply of the designer drug known as Wicked. After the close call he'd had the last time he'd started to get close, Nate couldn't afford any more slipups. Had Carson recognized him?

Nate didn't think so. He'd been working deep undercover inside a sign manufacturing company the last time either Carson brother had seen him. After his cover had been blown there, Nate had needed to move and had acquired a new cover.

He'd shaved the beard he'd had at the sign company, and traded his industrial uniform shirts and work pants for his usual attire—jeans and a wardrobe that consisted mostly of black. He was here in Treasure Point, a location he'd chosen for several strategic reasons, pretending to be working as a freelance photographer.

It was more free-form, less deep cover than he was used to. He was going by his own name. Only his occupation was a fabrication—and even so, photography was a real hobby of his. It was a risk, sticking close to his true identity, but in a small town where strangers were scrutinized closely, he'd felt it was worth it to stay as close to the truth as possible, so as not to tip people off that he was anything other than what he appeared to be.

That morning he'd been all over town taking pictures, and then he'd met with his informant. Jenni had been working with him and the rest of the GBI team for about half the time he'd been on the Carson case. She was a waitress here in Treasure Point and was trying to pull herself out of a life that had involved too many drugs and too much partying in the city on the weekends.

She'd caught the eye of a man with rumored ties to the Carson brothers' operation, and in an attempt to impress her, the man had told her more than he should have of the ins and outs of the organization. She'd brought the information straight to the GBI, and they'd had her continue to date the source and find out what information she could. She'd ended the relationship a few months back when her boyfriend had gotten violent with her, but by then she had enough contacts in the organization to continue providing the GBI with a steady stream of information.

Nate kept himself on alert as he made his way back to the room where he was staying. He paused in front of Claire's shop, Kite Tails and Coffee, and noted that everything looked undisturbed there—no indication that anyone had attacked her shop or her apartment upstairs in her absence. Ideally she would be safe when she made her way home after reporting the attack to the police. Nate wished he had her number to check on her, but he doubted she'd welcome hearing from him, anyway. She hadn't recognized him, not in the week he'd been in town—though he'd admittedly kept a low profile and only come into her shop for coffee at the busiest times of day because he wasn't ready for her to know who he was yet. He wasn't ready tonight, either.

He'd have to tell her, soon. No way to guess if the revelation about who he was would make her more or less likely to welcome him checking up on her, making sure she stayed safe.

Maybe that wasn't his job, anyway. Technically, according to the Georgia Bureau of Investigation, his job was to come to coastal Georgia, where the Carson brothers had spent the most time lately, track them down, track their movements, and figure out how they were transporting their supply of Wicked and where it was coming from. Nate didn't know at this point whether they were getting it from a middleman working as a transporter and supplier, or from the maker of the drug itself, but he'd work up from whatever he found. They wanted the people responsible for the drug's manufacture, and they wanted production halted. It was too dangerous, made people incredibly high and unusually strong. It lasted less than an hour for most people, but that time frame was intense. Some people died from the high itself, some from a reaction if the drug was used with alcohol. Some, feeling invincible from the strength the drug provided, put themselves in dangerous situations that caused their deaths or the deaths of others. Some people killed others under its influence.

Just outside the downtown business district of Treasure Point, movement in the shadows around a small apartment complex caught his eye. Nate put his hand to his hip almost unconsciously, felt the reassuring bulk of his sidearm concealed under his jacket. He always hoped he wouldn't have to use it, but as a certified peace officer, he was still law enforcement, and if it came down to needing to save lives, he'd pull out his weapon if he had to.

But for the sake of his cover? So much better if he didn't.

Nate moved closer to the apartment complex, sought his own shadows to hide himself, and he edged closer to where he'd seen movement.

A muffled scream caught his attention. One unit down, Nate thought. Maybe upstairs? He'd already started that way, picking up his pace, when he heard the two shots.

Some incorrectly called them silencers. In truth, it was a suppressor. And it didn't muffle the shots of a handgun enough for someone like him not to recognize it.

He was sprinting now, around the side of the building, dodging a trash can, and heading up the stairs. He heard glass shatter once he rounded the first level of the staircase. Likely the shooters were escaping from whatever apartment they'd been in. He couldn't chase them now, not when he knew they'd shot someone in this complex. His first duty was to check on the condition of whoever might have been hurt. Many gunshot wounds didn't have to be fatal if they were treated right away.

After rounding one more half flight of stairs, he arrived on the second floor, Nate hesitated. Up one more level? Or this one? He looked down into the sheltered hallway. Glass had shattered, meaning someone had escaped via the window. The person escaping must have expected to make it out okay and relatively quickly. Not the third floor.

He moved to the first door and had lifted his hand

to knock, since he couldn't very well break down any doors, when he saw that the door two doors down was open.

"Hello?" he called as he unholstered his gun, keeping it pointed safely at the ground, but both hands holding it tight, ready to pull it up if he needed it.

Nothing, no sounds at all. This apartment had lights on, as though someone was home. When he stepped inside, he saw that the TV was on, but with the sound muted. He swept his gaze left and right in the entryway. No signs of anything amiss here, but he knew what he'd heard and was almost certain that somewhere in this building, someone needed help.

His gaze caught on a purse on the entry table. It was a unique bright orange color. He recognized it as the same one Jenni had been carrying last time he'd seen her.

The adrenaline swirling through him mixed with dread as realization started to churn in his gut. This was Jenni's apartment.

Moving with more urgency, Nate cleared the living room, then the kitchen. He was growing more concerned about Jenni by the second, more convinced that she had been the target of those gunshots, and more worried that she'd been hurt.

Nate rounded the corner into the hallway. Two bedrooms, one on each end. He checked the first and found it empty. Down the hall, into the second.

Nate had to swallow hard. Jenni lay on the floor, blood pooled under her. He confirmed the room was empty of any threats as he approached her—noting the broken window in the back that had no doubt served as an escape route. There was a bit of blood on the glass, and he hoped that could get them some DNA they could use, although Nate was already relatively sure this was connected to what had happened to Claire earlier, and therefore connected to the Carson brothers.

Fighting the urge to be sick to his stomach at what he was seeing—death never got any easier—he reached his hand to Jenni's carotid artery to check for a pulse.

Nothing. It had been what he'd expected, but he'd owed it to her to check. She'd been a sweet girl, and extraordinarily brave—choosing to step up to help the investigation even though she knew it put her at risk. They should have been able to keep her safe. *He* should have been able to protect her. And he knew that failure would weigh on him for a long time.

Nate stepped back, positioned himself so that he could see through the door and through the window in case the shooter came back, and pulled his phone from his pocket.

"I need to report an apparent homicide."

TWO

The Treasure Point Police Department wasn't somewhere Claire had spent much time. She was thankful for its presence in her little town, and for the men and women who worked there, but it had never had much personal impact on Claire's life, beyond the time her sister had spent talking to the people here. She'd been the victim of several attacks, and then she'd married Matt and would occasionally come to the station to visit during his shifts.

Now, as she took a deep breath and squared her shoulders before walking in, Claire found herself hoping that this would be both the first and last time she had any need to go inside the building.

"This way," Matt directed her once they'd entered and moved through the open entryway. He motioned down a hall and then stopped in front of a door on the left, gesturing for her to precede him.

The room was nice enough. Not an interrogation room, at least not like any she'd seen on TV. There was a table and some chairs, but also a coffeemaker on a counter in the corner.

"Make yourself comfortable," Matt said as he moved

toward the coffeemaker. "Coffee? It's nowhere near as good as yours, but it'll warm you up if you're feeling chilled."

"No thanks." Claire settled into one of the chairs.

The radio on Matt's belt crackled, startling Claire. "Just ignore it," Matt said. "I have to keep it on. Sorry about that."

"It's okay."

The radio crackled again. More chatter. Claire wasn't paying much attention.

Not until she heard the word *homicide*.

Her head swung left. "What did they say?"

Matt reached for the radio, turned it up.

"…Egret Cove Apartments, white female, early twenties. BOLO out for a man involved in a downtown attack earlier. Suspect for that is in his early to midthirties, medium build, dark hair, dark eyes. Suspect is not a local."

When the radio crackled to white noise again, Claire spoke up. "Two women attacked in one night?"

"And one of them dead." Matt shook his head.

"Coincidence?"

"We can only hope so."

The door opened just then, and the chief, a man in his late fifties with gray hair and a full beard, entered the room. He came to her shop now and then for coffee during the day, usually mumbling disparaging remarks about whoever made the coffee at the police station.

"Hello, sir," she greeted him.

Matt looked at her with raised eyebrows. Claire shrugged. Was she not supposed to talk until he did? How was she supposed to know how it worked, being questioned?

"Claire. I'm glad to see you're okay." The chief took a seat at the end of the table.

"Thank you, sir. I'm glad to *be* okay."

"Can you tell me about what happened tonight?" He focused his attention her, leaned back in his chair a little.

"Sure. I was walking to the Christmas tree lighting. I was supposed to meet my sister there, and I was planning to tell her that lately I'd felt..." Claire trailed off, feeling foolish over what she was about to say, even after what had happened. Even knowing she'd been attacked, the idea of someone watching her seemed ridiculous. It was Treasure Point. It had its share of crime just like anywhere, but she'd never heard of there being problems of the stalker sort.

"Go on," the chief encouraged her.

"Lately I've felt like someone is watching me. Not all the time, just sometimes. Nothing's happened, so I figured it was probably just my imagination. But I felt that way tonight, and then not long into my walk, someone grabbed me from behind."

"Did he make any moves to hurt you physically?"

Claire shook her head. "No, besides his grip on my arms, and then his hand over my mouth, I didn't have any sense that he was trying to...kill me or do anything else. It felt more like he was planning to take me somewhere."

"And why didn't he succeed?"

"Another man ran over and told him to let me go. I didn't quite recognize him, but his voice seemed familiar. He fought off the attacker, reminded me to call the police and told me to go inside one of the stores."

A few seconds of silence passed. Then the chief looked to Matt. "She's met *him*."

Matt nodded. "I thought so, but wanted to see what you thought."

"I've met *who*? Who is he?"

Claire was glancing back and forth between both men, so it wasn't difficult for her to catch the slight head shake the chief gave to Matt. They weren't willing to tell her who he was yet, but neither of them seemed worried that she'd met him, so maybe he was on their side?

"So, what do I do? Is it okay for me to go home?"

Both men nodded.

"I don't see any reason you shouldn't," the chief began. "Right now we have no reason to believe your attack was anything but a random crime downtown. Sad, but it does happen. Take precautions, make sure your doors are locked tight, and let us know if you think someone is watching you again, but I don't expect you to have any more trouble. Matt can take you home now if you're ready to go. That's all we need from you for tonight. We'll be in touch if we need anything else." The chief stood, approached the coffeepot, then shook his head and turned away from it.

"I don't guess you'd want to make us some good coffee before you go?" The chief smiled and held up a hand when Claire moved in that direction. "I'm teasing you. Don't make any coffee. I've got to head to a murder scene. But if you want to have a cup ready for me tomorrow morning early, I'll pick one up before our morning roll call."

"I'll do that, sir."

Claire and Matt walked out of the room and made their way through the building to Matt's car parked outside. "Do me a favor and call Gemma to explain what happened?" he said. "That way I don't have to try to answer all of her questions when I get home."

"Scared of your own wife?" Claire teased, though she couldn't say she really blamed him. Gemma could be rather determined when she wanted something, like answers. She pulled her phone out. She did need to tell her sister what had happened.

She took a deep breath, braced herself for the conversation.

When Gemma answered the phone, Claire opened with "First, you need to know that I'm fine," hoping that the chief was right and this would be an isolated incident. If things got more dangerous, Claire knew she could count on Matt and Gemma's overprotection.

What scared her was the thought that she might actually need it.

As protocol dictated, Nate hadn't touched Jenni's body since he felt for a pulse and found none. He hadn't moved her at all, and she still lay there, stretched across the floor, looking so innocent in death, as his sister had. Murder was evil, never justified. And whoever the faceless man or woman who had pulled the trigger on Jenni turned out to be, the killer wasn't the real villain Nate was ultimately after. *That* was the entire illegal drug industry itself. It bore a lot of the responsibility for deaths like this one. Like his sister's.

He looked out the shattered back window again. Still nothing from there. It didn't appear that the shooter was coming back, which was logical. He'd finished the job.

Nate shook his head, moved his eyes quickly over Jenni's body as he looked back toward the front of the apartment. The police should be here any moment.

"Police!" an authoritative voice announced, followed by the sound of people coming inside. Nate couldn't see them yet, but he judged by the footsteps that there were several of them.

He recognized the police chief—his presence at a crime scene might have been unusual in a city, but it wasn't as surprising in a small town that probably didn't even see a murder every year.

"Agent Torres." The chief nodded like he wasn't surprised Nate had been the one to make the call. Nate liked the chief well enough, had had coffee with him when he first got to town to read him in on the GBI's case. When he'd worked deep cover in the past, that kind of cooperation with law enforcement hadn't been possible, but since this cover was less about embedding with drug runners and more about blending in to the background in Treasure Point long enough to get the evidence his team needed, Nate and his boss back in Atlanta had decided that working with the police department was better than not.

"Chief."

"I'm sorry it took us a couple of extra minutes to get here. I needed to listen to what happened to our town's coffee shop owner earlier this evening." He surveyed Nate, then caught his gaze and wouldn't let it go. "Would you know anything about that?"

"I might, sir."

"We'll talk more about that later." The chief moved toward Jenni's body, which one of the officers with him was photographing. "How did you know Jenni?"

Nate might have read the police department in on why he was in town, but he hadn't told them about Jenni. It was too risky to discuss it, since confidential informants all too often ended up dead. "She was my CI."

"Makes sense."

"She was helping me get more intel on my case. She knew some people with loose ties to the organization," Nate finished.

The chief nodded. "I'm sorry this happened."

"Me, too."

Nate turned to the door when he heard more footsteps.

It was a woman dressed in dark coveralls. "No one better have touched my crime scene."

"About time," the chief said to the woman. She raised her eyebrows, didn't back down in the face of the chief's bravado at all.

"I got caught behind the train." She seemed to take in the room, all the people working. Then her eyes landed on Nate. "I'm Shiloh Cole, crime scene investigator. Did you find the body?"

"Yes, I did. Nate Torres." He lowered his voice. "GBI, but I'm keeping that quiet."

"Good to meet you." She looked over at Jenni. "And this is?"

"Jenni was my CI. I'm afraid she got too close to some answers I needed about how the drug smuggling ring I'm tracking is transporting their merchandise, and who their supplier is. Either that or they found out she was feeding me information about them in general.

"Could be either."

Shiloh had a notepad out and was sketching the layout of the crime scene, including approximate distances. Then, starting at one side of the room, she started giving orders, having men bag up things she thought might be evidence, and getting out a crime scene kit herself. She dusted for fingerprints—high-traffic areas especially, but also a few places she could get good prints in general.

As she worked the rest of the crime scene in silence, Nate's respect for her grew. He hadn't been sure what to expect from a small-town crime scene investigator, but she was good at this.

He appreciated being allowed to stay, even if they were keeping what they found quiet, not showing him much. Ideally he'd find out more tomorrow. For now he kept his hands in his pockets and tried not to get in the way at all while he thought about the horrible turn this day had taken. Jenni's death was tragic, but the fact that she was killed on the same night Claire Phillips was attacked couldn't possibly be a coincidence—and it might mean he was closer to a breakthrough on this case than he had realized. Interested parties had most likely noticed his presence in Treasure Point, and it was making someone very nervous. Maybe this meant he was close to seeing the fruits of almost eighteen months focusing on the same case with hardly any break.

Tomorrow he'd go to Claire Phillips's coffee shop. First he'd make sure she was okay after the attack. She'd seemed like it, but his mind kept replaying how pale her face was, how wide her eyes were.

And then he'd try to figure out what the connection was between the attack against Claire and Jenni's death. Because he wasn't letting another woman die on his watch.

THREE

It wasn't too late when Matt dropped her off, so Claire locked the door behind herself as she'd promised to and fixed herself some dinner. If someone had asked, she wouldn't have said she was hungry, but apparently the experience earlier that evening hadn't robbed her of her appetite. It had done the opposite—she ate like she hadn't eaten all day.

After eating dinner, Claire cleaned up. Not just her kitchen, but the entire apartment. She fielded two more calls from Gemma since their phone conversation in the car, but Claire kept those talks pretty short. She just told her sister to listen to Matt, who had agreed with the chief that the attack was likely random.

At ten o'clock, Claire still believed that the police officers were right, that she was safe now. But she wasn't having any success convincing herself to become tired. Every time she so much as looked toward the bedroom, she knew there was no way sleep was coming, not anytime soon. So Claire did what she always did when some aspect of her life overwhelmed her and needed sorting out somehow.

She pulled out her box of painting supplies, dug

through until she came up with the watercolors. This was her preferred medium, especially when reality felt a little too harsh and needed the edges blurred slightly, the best light put on it. Tonight was a watercolor night if she'd ever seen one.

On a sheet of watercolor paper, she started to paint from a photo she'd taken of the marsh earlier in the week. As she did, she thought about what had happened tonight.

She'd been attacked. She let her mind wrap itself around that as she worked on blending just the right shade for the salt water in the marsh creek she was painting in the corner of the paper. She'd been attacked, but she didn't know why. Someone had rescued her, but while he looked familiar, she didn't know who he was. Not long after her attack, another woman in Treasure Point had been killed.

Claire was starting to question her decision to spend the night alone in her apartment. She knew Gemma or Matt would come get her if she asked, but was it really necessary? Murder in town or not, her random attacker wouldn't follow up, wouldn't track her down to her home.

Right?

Too many questions. And Claire didn't have the answers, something that didn't sit well with her. She always had the answers. She focused on her painting again, creek complete, and moved on to the delicate strokes that would make the marsh grass itself.

Claire glanced at the clock once or twice as she worked. Ten thirty. Then just past midnight. Her mind still wasn't tired. It was still racing with curiosities and possibilities.

She shivered, unable to shake the feeling of unease that had persisted since the attack. She set the brush down. Almost unconsciously she rubbed her left shoulder, the first place the man had grabbed. When she realized what she was doing, she jerked her hand away, like acknowledging the bruise somehow made what had happened more real. Instead of dwelling on it, she examined her painting—almost finished—to judge her progress so far.

It looked like the scene she'd seen and photographed, but the early morning sun had been warm in that picture, comforting and full of the promise of what the day would bring.

She'd stayed true to the water and the grass in that picture. The scene itself was exactly the same. But a change in the mood had come across through shadows, a bit of a feeling of discord in the particular shade of yellow-gold she'd chosen for the light. It wasn't the first time she'd done that, projected emotions she was feeling onto a painting, but it was certainly telling of how troubled she truly was by her attack. She kept painting anyway—it was beautiful even if it wasn't the picture she'd intended to paint. And it was helping her calm down—the subtle shaking of her hands that hadn't stopped since everything had happened was finally starting to ease.

Forty minutes after midnight, she set the brush down, painting complete. The idea of starting another crossed her mind, since usually she painted until everything in her mind was resolved, but she knew better than to expect to clear her mind fully after everything that had happened tonight. For now she did feel better, at least a little, and she needed to go to sleep, since she had to be downstairs at five o'clock to start the cinnamon rolls. Claire knew that bakeries in bigger cities opened so early that proprietors had to start baking at four or even three in the morning. But Treasure Point didn't get going until about seven most days. And even that was early for all but some fisherman and a few professionals whose jobs started early.

Claire put her paints away in order, the way she liked them, then stood and stretched. She looked around the nearly dark room and wished she'd turned a few more lights on. She had one small light on in the kitchen, her lamp on her painting table, and then the string of Christmas lights outside. The rest was darkness.

She usually turned off everything but the Christmas lights when she went to bed. Tonight she was leaving all of it on. She walked around the apartment, checking corners and closets even as she laughed at herself for her paranoia. If someone had been out to get her and hiding in her apartment, he'd have made his move to attack her when she was immersed in her painting.

Once she'd confirmed that she was the only one in the apartment and all the doors and windows were locked, Claire went to bed. *God, keep me safe*, she prayed as she started to drift.

Her eyes snapped open. Claire glanced at the clock. Just after two. It felt like she'd just fallen asleep, but apparently she'd gotten a couple of hours' worth.

She swallowed hard and looked around. Her room was dark, but the main living area still gave off a bit of light, enough for her to glance around and confirm that everything was undisturbed. She didn't know what had awakened her, but clearly there was nothing to worry about.

Claire settled back on her pillow, took a deep breath.

And with no warning, no flicker like a regular power outage often gave, the apartment went dark. And the stillness suddenly felt…not as empty as it had seconds before.

Like she wasn't alone.

The shadows in the darkness changed ever so slightly. Claire blinked. And then, in the slivers of moonlight that came through the cracks in the curtains in her bedroom window, she saw a shape.

Someone was in her bedroom.

Always go with your first instinct. It was one of the rules Nate tried to live by. But Nate had broken that rule when he'd pushed away the urge to visit Kite Tails and Coffee and check on Claire when he'd left Jenni's apartment. He'd wanted to make sure she was settled in safely for the night, but he'd felt drained after the long evening and had decided that checking in on her could wait until morning. He glanced at the red numbers of the hotel alarm clock. It was 2:00 a.m.

Closer to morning than nighttime.

Nate closed his eyes, forced his head a little deeper down into the pillow as though that would somehow help him forget the reason he wasn't sleeping and make rest come more easily. Not two minutes passed before he got up, threw on yesterday's jeans and then zipped his black leather jacket over the undershirt he'd been sleeping— well, trying to sleep—in. He'd walk downtown and confirm that things were quiet in the area around Claire's shop, and then maybe his mind would let him catch at least a couple of hours of good sleep before he went back into town in the morning to observe.

A week, he thought to himself as he quickened his pace on his course toward the middle of town. He'd been sitting in Kite Tails and Coffee every day for a week, watching people in the town come and go, and so far, he'd seen nothing that would help him with his case. On the bright side, Nate had a pretty good idea of folks' routines now. He'd always left the coffee shop when the morning rush died down around ten in the morning and walked around the town and the surrounding areas, taking pictures since being a photographer was part of his cover. He'd always wanted to delve deeper into the hobby, get better at it, and he should have been thankful for the time to do so.

Mostly, though, he'd be thankful for a break in this case. He had to be getting close to something or Jenni wouldn't have been targeted. And somehow it was connected to Claire, since she appeared to be a target, as well. But how? He didn't have all the pieces yet.

He was in Treasure Point to figure out where the supply of Wicked, the Carson brothers' drug of choice, was coming from. He didn't believe they were manufacturing it, but the brothers were good at making it look like they had no associates. That was why they'd become so important in the drug trade—people appreciated their discretion. But sooner or later, they'd slip up—and then, if it all went according to plan, they'd lead him to even bigger players in the trade.

The lights from downtown grew closer. Nate shook his head a little at the Christmas displays in the store windows. Not his favorite holiday. He felt that, as a Christian, maybe it should have been more special to him. And he was thankful for His salvation, thankful that Jesus coming as a baby made that possible.

But Christmas had been his sister's favorite holiday. And right now every single Christmas that passed without her just…hurt.

That was a subject he could wait for another time to think through. For now, better to push that one out of his mind and not think about it.

Instead he focused on what he was doing now. Coming down here to check on Claire had seemed like such a good idea when he'd been lying in his hotel room, unable to sleep. But now that he was here…what? Did he call her in the middle of the night, announce that he was the guy who'd rescued her and just hope she didn't flip out? How could he even explain how he had her number?

But standing here in the street near her building wasn't doing her any good, not really.

Nate spun on his heel, turned back in the direction he'd come from. Less than ten steps away, he stopped again. Something was wrong, but he couldn't put his finger on what. Then it hit him.

Claire's Christmas lights hadn't been on. In fact, the entire building had been dark, unlike the other shops downtown, most of which had at least a dim light on inside to discourage break-ins. The lights being off in the middle of the night wasn't necessarily reason enough to get concerned…but this wasn't his first late-night walk around the center of town, and he was almost certain that she'd had Christmas lights on then, hadn't she? Surely he would have noticed if there was just one shop that stayed completely dark.

Nate couldn't shake the worries that the darkness meant someone had flipped a breaker to cut her power. Something that would make it easier for someone to break into her apartment and catch her off guard.

His stomach churned. Gut instinct swirled against self-doubt, but instincts won and Nate turned around, walked to the front of the shop, tried the door.

Locked. Good, that was smart of her. Now was the part where he should turn *back* around and return to his hotel room. But he couldn't. Instead he found himself walking around the back of the building in search of a staircase. Many old downtown buildings had exterior fire escapes running down the back of the structure, supplying direct access into the living spaces above through a window or a sliding door. Surely if she'd been conscientious enough to lock the shop door, Claire had locked the door or window that opened out onto the fire escape. He'd check it and if it was locked, he'd head back to the hotel and laugh at his paranoia. If it wasn't secure…

Nate found the stairs, which appeared to lead up to a small deck, decorated with a patio table and a pair of chairs. Was the sliding door cracked open? Maybe. He couldn't be sure.

He took the steps up two at a time as the urgency to make sure she was safe built inside him. He made a quick scan of the deck. Nothing seemed off or out of place there. Nate made his way across the deck, straight to the door.

It stood open about an inch. She might have left it open like that herself…but when Nate pulled a small flashlight out of his pocket and shone it on the knob, signs of forced entry were evident.

It was too much like the situation with Jenni earlier. Too similar. His stomach sank as he thought of the time he'd wasted, second-guessing his decision to come and check on Claire. Was he about to discover that he had arrived too late yet again?

Nate swallowed hard as he pushed the door the rest of the way open. He'd never been in Claire's apartment, so he wasn't sure where he was going, but he felt along the wall on the right-hand side for a light switch. There. He flipped it on.

Nothing. Solid darkness everywhere.

Nate's suspicions were confirmed. Someone had flipped the breakers.

And chances were good that the attacker was in Claire's house or had been. "Claire!" he yelled.

A muffled scream came from one of the rooms further back. He started forward, pulling out a small flashlight from his pocket and shining it in front of him. The living room seemed to be empty. He kept running, past the kitchen, back to what he assumed were bedrooms.

He lifted his flashlight. It didn't do much to light up the entire room, but right now he didn't need it to. It shone directly onto a large figure that wasn't Claire.

And that was all Nate needed to see.

"Let her go!" he yelled as he moved forward, trying to catch sight of Claire. She must be on the other side of the intruder.

She was. Huddled on the bed against the wall, with a lamp lifted up. As soon as the intruder turned toward Nate, she took a swing, hard, and connected with his head. The assailant stumbled back, looked from Claire to Nate, and then shoved past Nate and ran out the door.

Nate hesitated. Stay with Claire or run? It was déjà vu from earlier in the evening.

"Go. I'm fine."

It was all he needed to hear. This time he ran, but catching up with the attacker wasn't as easy as he'd expected. The other man threw things in his path as he ran past them. Nate kept his footing but wasn't fast enough to close the distance between them. Just as the intruder was about to get away, Nate lunged, grabbed at him.

His hand latched on to something the man was wearing, but Nate tripped and fell on the ground, straight onto his knee. Nate's hand came away with only some kind of utility pouch that had been Velcroed onto the other man's belt as the intruder darted away. Nate opened it up. Just some tools, nothing incriminating, nothing that helped identify him. He'd give them to Shiloh to see if she could run them for prints, but with as much evidence as this case was giving her to process, he knew it would certainly take a few days, maybe even a few weeks.

He made a fist and hit the floor. Maybe if he'd acted sooner he could have avoided this altogether, kept the man from getting in.

For now, he'd done all he could. He staggered to his feet, wincing at the pain in his knee but relieved that it seemed only bruised, not sprained or torn. And at least Claire was safe. "He got away. I'm sorry," he called to her as he walked back in her direction, intentionally making as much noise as possible so that he wouldn't startle her. There was no telling how she'd be handling this…

He made his way back to her room, found her in the same place where he'd left her.

"Claire." He stopped in the doorway, watched her for some acknowledgment of his presence, but she said nothing, just sat there. "Claire, he's gone. You're okay."

Still nothing.

"All right, get up. You need to call the police."

At that, her gaze finally shot to him. The stunned look on her face, the vulnerable one that had started to rip his heart out, was replaced by sheer indignation.

Good. He'd made her mad, stopped her from panicking. It was what he'd been aiming for, even if it meant she thought he was a jerk now because of it.

She reached for a cell phone on the bedside table. Nate noted her hands were shaking. That would likely continue for the next little while.

"Hi, this is Claire Phillips. Someone broke into my apartment."

FOUR

Claire stood frozen in her living room, eyes glued to the view outside her window. It had seemed the only safe spot to look at, since her home was in shambles. The police were on their way, so for now all there was to do was wait.

She didn't know which was scarier—the fact that there had been an intruder in her home, or the fact that he had wreaked all this destruction while she'd been asleep and unaware, only waking up moments before the man actually entered her bedroom. The thought of someone going through her paint supplies, rifling through her stack of finished paintings…it was worse than just an invasion of privacy, more than vandalism.

"Are you okay?"

The solid but quiet voice of her rescuer was familiar, and not just from tonight. Claire's frowned as she looked up at him. Was it possible she knew him from somewhere other than the coffee shop?

To answer his question, she shook her head. No. She wasn't okay. But she didn't want to talk about that right now. "I know you," she said, studying his face as she took a step closer to him. "Where do I know you from? You aren't from Treasure Point."

"No," he admitted. "I'm not."

"You're not denying that I recognize you from some-where, though."

He shook his head slightly, then stilled, head tilted to the side just a little, as he studied her in return. "I rec-ognized you right away, but then again, you've changed less since college than I have."

"College..." she mumbled.

As though she'd summoned the memories up, a col-lage of snapshots from her college life played through her mind. She'd left Treasure Point for college, gone to Savannah to chase her big-city dreams just like any ste-reotypical small-town seventeen-year-old. She'd studied well, worked hard to keep her GPA up, but she'd also had fun with her group of friends. Kayaking near Little Tybee Island, climbing at the rock gym in Savannah... There had been a large group of them, but the three she'd spent the most time with were her roommate, Katie Dun-bar, her boyfriend at the time, Justin Colton...

And the man she now recognized as the one stand-ing in front of her. Nate Torres.

"Nate." She'd never thought she'd see him again, not after their group's friendship had fizzled after Justin had left for Atlanta to get his master's. The two of them had tried dating long-distance, but Justin had not been cut out for a committed relationship. At least, not with her. Claire had found that out the hard way when she'd shown up in Atlanta to surprise him one weekend and found that he was out with another woman. He'd apolo-gized and promised that it was an isolated mistake—that he'd never do it again. Like the naive girl she was then,

Claire had believed he meant it. Maybe he had. But their relationship had never been the same and then…then the accident had happened.

Dating Justin had been a risk in more than one way. A risk taken lightly that had ended badly.

Claire had learned her lesson, had matured past the attraction to charming bad boys since then. What she was looking for now was more along the lines of a steady, predictable man with a stable job. Someone mature, who realized that adventures were for kids, and adults had to settle down. Be dependable. Stay committed.

Though to be fair, a sensible, unadventurous guy wouldn't have been any use to her tonight. If someone steady and unexcitable had seen her getting attacked in the street, he'd have called the police or gone for help. He never would have directly charged her attacker to force him to release her. And breaking into her apartment to protect her from a dangerous intruder? Forget about it. For better or for worse, Nate was exactly what she'd needed tonight, and she was grateful that he'd been there for her—not just once, but twice.

And if he happened to look particularly handsome and heroic just now, she was just going to have to ignore it. Never again was she going to let attraction overpower her good sense.

Nate was the epitome of everything she'd never fall for again. But while he was the last man on earth she'd get involved with, he *was* someone she trusted.

Claire swallowed hard. "Nate," she repeated. "Do you want to tell me what you're doing in Treasure Point?"

"I'm here as a photographer."

"You're a photographer now?"

"It's one of the things I do, yes."

"And the others? Legal? Not legal?"

"Claire, you can trust me."

"Oddly enough, I know that. But I also know that it's too much of a coincidence that someone tried to kill me right after you came to town—and that you just happened to be in the right position to save me. Twice. There's something more going on here, isn't there?"

He didn't seem to see those words coming, and for a minute he didn't say anything, just stood there. Still and speechless.

"Yes, there's more going on here. But as for who wants you dead… I don't know why anyone would be after you."

"But I do."

Claire swung her gaze to the door, where two uniformed officers stood. Her brother-in-law, Matt, and his friend Clay.

"What do you mean?" she asked Matt.

He pulled out his phone, tapped the screen a few times and then held it up to show her a picture.

"That's my business card. For the shop." Claire shook her head. "You think someone wanted me dead because…"

"Wait, I wasn't done." Another few taps. He held up the phone again. "This is the back of the same business card."

Scrawled on the plain white card stock in a handwriting that she didn't recognize were two words. "What do these mean to you?"

Ocean Lights.

"It's the painting I just finished last week."

"What was it of, Claire?"

"Just…just landscape, like all my paintings. You think

that's why someone wants me dead? That doesn't make any sense. It's a painting, Matt, not anything important." The words felt multilayered to Claire, like a betrayal of her true self even as they came out of her mouth. She'd like to think her paintings did have meaning, but for now they were a hobby. The coffee shop was her real business. And besides, what she'd really meant was that her paintings weren't anything to kill over.

That much she was sure of.

"This business card was found in the hands of a woman who was murdered here in Treasure Point earlier this evening."

The thought of a murder was horrifying—and more horrifying that it had been in Treasure Point. She'd heard about it on the police radio at the station, but it was fully sinking in now. What if it was someone she knew? Out of the corner of her eye, Claire noticed that Nate winced almost as much as she did. A visceral reaction…except his wasn't surprise.

Nate had already known about that murder?

She looked back at her brother-in-law. Looked back at Nate. She'd almost say from the way he had a habit of showing up and rescuing her, from the way he was hyperfocused on the crimes that had happened earlier, that he was law enforcement himself, but the black leather certainly didn't fit the clean-cut image she associated with the police in Treasure Point.

"Claire is going to need protection on her at all times," Nate stated.

"There's no need," Matt said. "They should have the guy by now. I got the call that he'd been found just after I received orders to come here."

Claire watched Nate for a reaction, but this time she got nothing but solid poker face.

"Who are they bringing in?"

"Trace Johnson, Jenni's ex-boyfriend. He'd been threatening her—she filed a complaint, was trying to get a restraining order."

"And you think he killed her and then came over here to kill Claire?"

Matt shook his head. "Listen, I'm not saying it makes complete sense yet. We're still working everything out. But it's possible. Who else would have a reason to be after Jenni?"

"The better question is, what reason would Jenni's ex-boyfriend have to go after Claire, just because Jenni had her business card?"

"We're going to be working the next few days on establishing motive as well as collecting more evidence. You know how this works, Torres. How about you do your job and let us do our jobs?"

Nate shook his head, and Claire recognized that stubborn set to his jaw. He was usually easygoing, but when he dug in his heels, he was unmovable. "I think she needs protection until you can prove he was behind both crimes. Or either crime, for that matter."

"She's my sister-in-law. I want her safe, too, but we have no reason to think Trace isn't our guy."

"We'll talk more about this later." Nate's voice left no doubt that he meant it. The conversation wasn't over.

Claire's gaze bounced between the two men, one who she knew cared about her like family, and the other who should have just been part of a past she'd almost forgotten about, but had turned up back in her life and was now making it very clear that he would fight for her safety.

But why did he care so much? And why was he so convinced she was still in danger from her attacker when Matt and Clay seemed to think she wasn't?

Nate Torres knew more than he was letting on.

She thought of Matt's words just now. "You do your job and let us do our jobs…" Was he talking about the photography business? Somehow Claire didn't think so. She needed answers. And it seemed like Nate might be the one who could give them to her.

"You're not staying here for the rest of the night," Nate said to Claire once the officers had moved into the bedroom to see if the intruder had left behind any evidence.

"Excuse me?" She raised her eyebrows. "I don't think that a few years of friendship nearly a decade ago entitles you to tell me how to live my life. If the police don't think it's safe for me to stay, then that's one thing, but who are you to tell me it's not?"

Something in her eyes… This wasn't just bravado. She was genuinely asking, challenging him to give her an answer—to explain what he was doing in town, and what his connection was to the attacks against her.

He'd known when it became apparent that the Carson brothers were using Treasure Point for some of their operations that coming to town and using it as his base to investigate meant running into Claire was inevitable. Thankfully, for the last couple of weeks she hadn't recognized him, and he didn't blame her. He'd changed since college, a transformation that had begun his senior year when his younger sister died, and that had continued until he was the guy he was now.

The guy he was now knew the dangers of letting

anyone get close to him. It didn't just risk his secrets—
which could mean life or death for an undercover agent.
It also put his heart at risk of getting hurt. And he'd
shouldered too much hurt already to sign himself up
for another dose.

Nate looked away from Claire before those enormous
brown eyes could get to him any more. She trusted him,
she said. Well, she shouldn't. His sister had, and yet he
hadn't managed to say anything to convince her to leave
the path she'd put herself on—the one that had led to her
death. Jenni had trusted him, too, and she'd bled out on
the floor of her apartment earlier.

He wished he could tell Claire to quit trusting him.

Although his investigation would be easier if she did.
And more important if he looked at it logically, she'd
be more likely to stay safe if she'd follow his advice.
Not that that made him feel much better about her odds.

"Why don't you ask what you really want to know,
Claire?" He met her eyes again, tried to steel himself
better against their effect on him this time.

"I want to know who you really are."

No, she didn't, not who he was in his core. But that
wasn't what she was asking. She wanted to know why
he was in town, what he was doing in Treasure Point.

Those kinds of questions, he was prepared to answer.
He'd talked to his supervisor at the GBI, Wade Beckett,
soon after he came to town, and let him know that he
had a history with someone in Treasure Point. She might
have questions if she recognized him. After conducting
a thorough background check on her, Wade had agreed
that if it became necessary to tell Claire why Nate was
in town in order to maintain his cover with everyone
else, then it was okay.

That didn't mean Nate was ready for her to know.

But her gaze wasn't letting up, and when it came down to it…Nate knew who was after her.

And she needed to know if she was going to stay alive.

"I'm an agent with the Georgia Bureau of Investigation. I'm in Treasure Point undercover to do recon on a drug smuggling group that we believe is operating in the area."

Whatever she'd been expecting, it obviously hadn't been that. He watched her blink a few times, and then she moved to the couch. Sank down into it.

"How much are you allowed to tell me?"

So she understood the basic parameters of secrecy his job demanded. That was something *he* hadn't been expecting.

"Enough to give you an idea of who wants to kill you and how important it is that you take whatever precautions I suggest."

"Tell me."

"Tony and Jesse Carson are brothers. The GBI has been tracking them for the last eighteen months because of their involvement in the distribution of a new designer drug, Wicked. Recently they moved their operations down to somewhere south of Savannah, most likely because the country down here is more difficult to track people in. Swamps, marshes, gators… There are a lot of places to get lost between Savannah and the Georgia-Florida line."

"So what exactly are you here to find out?"

"We don't know right now if the Carsons are manufacturing and distributing the drug, or if they're working with someone else to make it, or if they're taking orders from someone. My gut tells me that there's a higher-up calling the shots. If we can gather enough evidence against the Carsons, they might roll over and sell out the guy who's running the show."

"But either way, the Carsons are the ones who want me dead?"

"It looks that way, yes. The man who attacked you on the street—I recognized him. It was Jesse Carson himself. He must have a reason to have attacked you personally rather than sending one of his thugs to do it. It might have been him in the apartment tonight, too, though I can't be certain."

"And the woman earlier. The one who was killed. You think she fits into this, too, don't you?"

He nodded slowly. "Apparently the police don't agree with me, though. Maybe they're right. Maybe it's just a coincidence that her ex happened to get violent on the same night the Carson brothers wanted to take you out… but I doubt it."

"Was she…were you…?"

Nate shook his head, knowing what she was asking. "She was my confidential informant."

"But why would someone kill her?"

"If they found out she was giving information to law enforcement, that would be reason enough—these guys don't take betrayal lightly. But there's also the possibility that she found out something important, and they wanted to silence her to keep her from telling anyone."

"And why did she have my business card?"

"I don't know. But wait, as long as we're talking about that, what was written on the back? You said it was the name of a painting, right?"

Claire nodded. *"Ocean Lights."*

"Is it downstairs in your shop?" He'd noticed the gallery wall of artwork displayed the first time he'd been in the shop. Claire was a talented woman—but then, he'd always known that.

"No." Her eyebrows pushed together as she frowned. "That's why it seems odd she'd have the name of that one."

"You haven't told anyone about it?"

"I told Gemma the other day when we were having lunch at the diner."

Even without knowing how the painting fit into this, Nate could feel tension building in his neck and shoulders. Of course Claire would have had no reason to realize it wasn't safe to talk about her latest painting in a public place, but now that it *did* have significance and a connection to at least one serious crime, it was a privacy nightmare. Literally anyone could have heard her having that conversation. They'd get no leads from pursuing that.

Nate would deal with the implications later. For now, he needed to know more.

"What made this piece special?"

"Here, I can show you." Claire stood, moved toward the paintings stacked against the side wall of her living room, started to flip through them.

She got to the last one, stilled. And then started over.

Nate knew where this was going but asked anyway. "What is it?" He moved closer to her, protective instincts amping up even more at the repeated reminders that someone had been in her house.

"It's gone."

"You didn't misplace it." It was more a statement than a question.

Claire shook her head.

"Someone took it tonight."

"How long was he in here before I woke up? What else did he do?" She muttered the words softly, but Nate still caught them. Looking paler by the moment, Claire sunk down onto the couch again.

"There's no way to tell."

A tear ran down Claire's cheek. Nate moved closer, not sure what he could do to help, but feeling like he should at least try. More than one tear. Several.

She sniffed and brushed at her cheek. "I just don't understand."

Was she more upset about the painting or the home invasion? He didn't feel like he could fix it, at least *try* to fix it, until he knew. "Don't understand..." he prompted her.

"What does your case or the woman who was killed have to do with my painting? Even if she overheard me talking about it, why would she care?"

"Can you tell me more about the painting?"

Claire was staring at the painting table, seeming lost in thought. After a minute, she looked back at him. Met his eyes.

"Now that I know why you're here in town..." She shook her head, brushed another tear away. "I'm afraid I did something stupid."

"On purpose?"

"Completely accidentally. But that doesn't put me in any less danger, does it?" Claire let out a breath, pushed herself up from the couch and started to pace. "I've been having trouble sleeping lately."

"Something wrong?"

"Just a lot on my mind. Watching the ocean usually

calms me down, so I often go out onto the deck and just watch it, listen to the waves. With the rest of this area mostly abandoned at night, it's quiet. Peaceful."

"So what did you do that was stupid?"

Claire exhaled. "One night, very late, I saw lights from where I stood on the deck, lights on the ocean like they belonged to a boat. But it's not normal in this area for people to have boats out on the water in the middle of the night, so I'd never seen the way the lights reflect off the waves and mix with the moonlight before. I wanted to paint it."

"So that was the subject of your painting?"

Claire gave a nod. "Yes."

"You potentially painted a drug smuggling run, or a drug meet-up. I'm guessing with both of those, but I think it makes sense, Claire."

"It does, now that you've told me drug smuggling is happening in the area. At the time, I didn't have a reason to think there was anything sinister about it. It's Treasure Point, and while we have had our share of crime lately, drug smuggling being a problem had never crossed my mind."

Claire looked sick, and Nate couldn't blame her. Her decision to paint some lights on the ocean, something seemingly innocuous, had put her life at risk.

All they could do now was damage control. It was too late to change the past.

Just then one of the officers strode out of the bedroom, looked over at Claire. "Matt is helping Shiloh process the scene. But I'm supposed to tell you that you'll be staying at Matt and Gemma's house tomorrow—well, today, technically. It's Matt's scheduled day off, and that will give you some protection."

Claire nodded, glanced over at Nate.

"If it's okay, I'd like to ask you a few more questions myself," he said. "Dinner?"

She nodded. "I can do dinner. Since I'm assuming you're armed…" Her eyes moved to his hip, and while Nate knew his .40 was completely concealed, he was impressed that she'd guessed correctly right where it was. "Maybe you could bring me back over here to clean up some of this mess after we eat? I'm not going to be staying here anytime soon, but I'd feel better knowing there wasn't a huge mess. Or we could come here and I'll cook—it'll mean we're not out at a restaurant some-where we might be easy to attack."

"If that works for the chief." Nate looked back at the chief.

He nodded. "Sounds like a good plan. I'll have offi-cers here processing the scene for the next few hours, but we'll lock it up after we're done. There shouldn't be any need for you to stay out or leave things as they are once evidence has been logged. We should be able to get everything we need before noon, I would guess."

"Thank you." Claire shook her head. "I can't believe this is all happening. And wait, what about my shop? I can't just close for the duration of…whatever this is."

"We understand that." Nate thought he spoke for all of them. "But tomorrow is rather critical. Both attacks on you have been so close together that the chances of another one goes down with every hour that passes to-morrow, if that makes sense. Basically, someone wanted you taken out tonight. So either they're going to hit hard again as soon as they can to get rid of you as quickly as possible, or they've decided to step back and regroup before targeting you any further. We won't know which strategy they've chosen until we see how it plays out. So for tomorrow, we want someone with you one hundred percent of the time."

There was a hint of the old Claire in the way she physically cringed at the idea of full-time protection. She'd been so independent in college—that clearly hadn't changed. But she'd also been such a free spirit, confident and adventurous. How she'd gone from that to running a coffee shop and living the life of someone much older, he had no idea.

FIVE

Claire had anticipated a much more awkward day, considering that she wasn't allowed to leave Matt and Gemma's house. Not only that, she was only allowed to leave her brother-in-law's sight for five minutes at a time, and that was only to use the restroom. But Matt and Gemma made the day fun. They played multiple rounds of a board game they all liked, Claire helped Gemma organize some of her kitchen cabinets, and then they watched a movie in the afternoon.

Nate picked her up in her car just before five and drove her back to her apartment. Surprisingly, Claire hadn't felt any signs of fear at being back. No, the only fear she was feeling right now stemmed from anxiety about this evening itself, about what it would be like to be alone with Nate, someone who knew the *old* Claire. What did he think of her now that she'd come running back to her hometown, back to the "safe" life she'd claimed to be trying to escape back in her college days?

She reminded herself that it didn't matter what he thought. All that mattered was the fact that his presence meant she could be here, cleaning up this mess after she fed them both something, and that he might give her a clearer picture of how the events of yesterday affected her life, at least temporarily. Her safety was at stake here. That was far more important than her pride, no matter how much it smarted to have him see how much she'd changed.

Claire unlocked the door, and Nate followed her inside. She found it ironic that though she made her living with hospitality downstairs at the coffee shop, she rarely had people over to her apartment. She'd had friends over more often before she'd sold her house. The apartment just wasn't very conducive to having guests. But her options for people to entertain were dwindling, anyway, unless she wanted to be the third wheel—the only person not part of a couple. She had friends in town from high school, but most of them were married by now, and several of them had kids. She knew, theoretically, that she should still maintain relationships with them, but tell that to the feeling of loneliness and overwhelming awareness of her table-for-one relationship status any time she'd tried in the past to have a couple over.

Lately it hadn't been worth it to her. She'd had her parents over, and Gemma and Matt, but that was it.

"You're sure you don't mind having dinner with me and talking about the case? I should have asked you in the car, I guess," Nate said as they walked inside, giving her an out she was all too tempted to take.

Honestly? No, Claire wasn't sure. But she still didn't feel like she understood what she was up against. Maybe she just needed Nate to rehash what he'd said last night, let her have a chance to process it when she wasn't sleep-deprived and pumped full of adrenaline from waking up to find someone in her apartment. Something still didn't make sense to her, and she couldn't put her finger on what it was.

Besides, there was that elusive feeling of safety that had been missing since yesterday when she was attacked in town. Something about Nate nearby brought that back, logical or not. Was it the fact that he was someone she had a history with? That didn't make much sense—she had a history of some type or another with almost everyone in this town, including just about everyone on the police force. She was surrounded by people who had known her forever.

So why did Nate affect her this way? Claire didn't know. But he did. She'd felt his absence all day—she wanted to feel safe now.

Which is why she said, "I'm sure," and put as much confidence into her voice as she could.

"All right. At least let me help make dinner, then. What are we having?"

And with that, Nate was in her kitchen, moving toward the sink, then washing his hands and standing ready to help like he belonged there. Anything Claire was lacking in confidence tonight she could borrow from Nate, because he had more than enough.

"I was thinking something simple. Okra and tomatoes with Cajun sausage and rice sound okay?"

Nate smiled. Had she seen him smile like that before? If she had, it had been a very long time ago—which was a shame. Because as attractive as he was when he looked serious and thoughtful—which was most of the time—he was at least as handsome when he smiled. "Sounds great."

Claire swallowed hard and looked away from him. "You can cut up the okra if you want. It's in the fridge, and cutting boards are in the second drawer to the left of the stove."

They worked together in silence for a little while, which went more smoothly than Claire would have expected. The only person who'd ever tried to cook in this kitchen with her was Gemma. She loved her sister, but she and Gemma had realized that they weren't meant to share the same kitchen. They ran into each other, reached over each other and got in the way so thoroughly that it took twice as long to cook anything. She and Nate moved through dinner prep like it was some kind of dance they'd both done before.

Dance? Really? Claire shook her head. Nate Torres was the last man on earth she should have such thoughts about. Dating Justin back in college had been a bad enough idea, and she'd sworn off anyone resembling that type ever since.

And Nate? Nate was so much *more* than everything that had made Justin wrong for her in the end—even without the long-distance aspect. Nate was the one who had always pushed their group to take bigger chances, go on more daring escapades. If Justin had been rock climbing and rappelling, taking calculated risks for the thrill of the adventure, Nate was skydiving, free-falling. All risk—no calculation involved. And given that he was choosing to work undercover for the GBI, it was clear that he hadn't changed a bit.

She needed to think about something else, and fast. Because even though her head was flashing every kind of warning sign it had, Claire had to admit that his black leather personality coupled with the fact that he kept showing up just in time to save her…it made her foolish heart skip here and there at his proximity, even though she knew nothing could ever come of it.

Conversation. That would give her something else to focus on. She searched for a safe subject, was startled at the words that tumbled out of her mouth. "I'm a little nervous about being here tonight…"

"With me?" He frowned. Not what she'd meant at all, although now that he brought it up…

"No, I just meant being here in my apartment. After everything that's happened."

"You're safe here with me."

She stirred the rice, started the okra and tomatoes, and whispered a prayer of thanks that Nate kept quiet after that. "Okay, it just needs a little while to simmer. Want to sit down?"

"Let's do that. Then maybe I can answer the questions you still have."

"Thanks." They moved to the living room, each taking opposite ends of the sofa, since Claire's only chair was stacked high with paintings they'd looked at last night. She glanced away from those as fast as she could. Had she really understood his explanation about his investigation correctly last night?

"Tell me one more time what you're doing here?"

He gave her many of the same details he'd given last night, about trying to watch the Carson brothers to see if they led to a drug's manufacturer or to any other major players in the drug scene that the GBI would want to take down.

"So basically," Claire interrupted when she didn't think she could handle any more details, "you're in town to figure out who's involved in a drug smuggling ring. And you think I saw them?"

"That basically sums it up."

"I liked my life better last week, when I was running the coffee shop, not worried about anything…" She trailed off, ashamed of the show of weakness around Nate, but unable to stop her emotions.

"You can handle it, though, Claire. We will do our best to wrap up the investigation as quickly and thoroughly as we can. For now, you'll have to take extra precautions, but soon you should have your life back. Just keep being brave until then."

"I'm afraid I wouldn't call myself brave."

"The girl I knew back in Savannah was incredibly brave."

"That's who I was, Nate. Not who I am." Claire shook her head. Nate's eyes didn't leave her face, and she could only imagine what he was thinking, how his opinion of her had changed. Disappointing people was Claire's kryptonite, and she couldn't take it tonight. She had to get out of here, get away from his gaze. It felt like he could see right through her. And actually, he probably could. "I'm going to go check on dinner."

She was out of the room in one quick motion. He'd rarely seen someone in such a hurry to escape.

Her absence gave him a minute to try to reconcile what he'd learned in the last hour with what he'd known of Claire a decade ago. When he'd come to Treasure Point, realized it was the same small town Claire had grown up in and obviously returned to, he'd initially thought her job at the coffee shop gave her an ideal position to serve as another informant to him, should that become necessary.

That was out of the question at this point, with Jenni's

death. He didn't need anyone else's death added to the list of things he was responsible for.

But even if he'd wanted Claire's help, Nate doubted she was up for it. She seemed to have created a life for herself here that was built around fitting in, playing it safe and never pushing the envelope. It was nothing like the life he would have pictured her wanting. But she clearly wasn't that person anymore. People changed.

He sure had. The kid he'd been in college, who'd sought out thrills for fun, for the adrenaline rush, had definitely changed. Danger wasn't *fun* anymore. It was a part of life that was necessary in his job to get justice for the people who needed it.

He never should have expected her to be the same person she'd been back then. Having her help with the investigation wasn't an option. In good news for her, there hadn't been the slightest threat against her today. The Carsons had apparently decided to leave her alone for now. And there was even a chance that they weren't behind Jenni's death after all, meaning his case might not have taken the turn toward the darker that Nate had feared.

The Treasure Point Police Department was sure that Jenni's ex-boyfriend was responsible for her death—a gunshot residue test from his hands had come back positive. His fingerprints had been found in several locations in the apartment, high-traffic places they shouldn't have been found if he hadn't seen Jenni since they'd broken up three months before. It really might end up being a coincidence that Jenni had been attacked on the same night as Claire after all. Then again, this boyfriend of Jenni's had ties to the Carsons. Maybe…maybe Nate should finish out this dinner and tell Claire no more than the bare minimum about his investigation that he'd already told her, just in case his gut instinct had been right and she was still in danger.

Then they could both get on with their lives—the ones he never would have guessed either of them would be living.

Nate stood, not sure he'd be much help since cooking wasn't his strong suit, but thinking he'd better go see if Claire needed anything.

He walked into the kitchen.

And dropped to the ground, right next to where Claire lay on the floor. "Claire!" he shouted, checking for signs of a pulse, feeling like this was too similar to what he'd done the day before with Jenni.

Unlike yesterday, though, there was no obvious indication of what had happened to Claire.

Nate still wasn't finding a pulse. He moved his hand a little, shifted to another position on her neck.

There. Thready, light, but there.

Thank You, Lord, he prayed even as he slid his phone from his pocket and called 911 for the second time in two days.

Things had been heating up with this case as he'd inched closer and closer to the Carson brothers, started to have a clearer picture of the fact that they might not be the head guys of the organization the GBI was targeting. But it had begun as a slow simmer, and last night had shifted to a full boil. He'd thought things had slowed back down today—but clearly he'd been wrong. "I need an ambulance downtown, to the apartment over Kite Tails and Coffee. It's Claire Phillips. She unresponsive."

Claire's breathing grew more shallow. He pressed the speaker button, threw the phone down and positioned

Claire's head the best he could to ensure that her airway was as open as possible. While this could be a natural health emergency, Nate doubted it. It was too big of a coincidence. Besides, something about her appearance was too much like his sister's had been. Whatever she'd taken… No, he didn't believe she'd taken anything. This was different than his sister's death. Whatever she'd been *given* was wreaking havoc on her.

Nate listened to her breathing, trying to decide if she was struggling enough to need rescue breaths. He looked her over and did a double take when he realized how quickly her color was turning dusky, headed toward purple as though death was already inevitable.

No, he wouldn't let it be. Not today.

Nate positioned himself over her, brought his face down to hers and gave her two rescue breaths. He checked her breathing again. Still the same. So was the color.

If anything, it was worse. And she hadn't moved at all.

Please, let her be okay.

As he watched, her coloring grew even more dusky. He put a hand on hers. Cold.

How much worse could she grow before whatever damage the drug was doing to her system was irreversible?

Nate heard the sirens in the distance as he started to give her CPR. *Please, let her be okay. Please, let her be okay.* He knew God heard the first time, but he couldn't stop repeating the prayer in time to the compressions he was administering.

Nothing seemed to be working.

The EMTs stormed in, two of them. One of them

dropped an emergency bag on the floor, immediately unzipped it and started unrolling a hose of some kind. For oxygen?

The hiss of the oxygen tank confirmed that for Nate. Both paramedics worked quickly, and he watched with relief as they inserted a tube into her mouth. One of them started to pump an Ambu bag that would allow her to breathe.

"What can you tell us?"

"Claire Phillips, age twenty-nine. I've been with her today since five o'clock. She was making dinner for us. Five minutes ago, she was fine—talking with me normally. Then she came in here, and…this is how I found her. Um, I'm afraid that's all I know."

"How did she become like this?"

"Not sure. I think she was poisoned."

One EMT looked up just long enough to frown. "With what?"

"If I had to guess… Wicked. It's a designer drug with narcotic characteristics."

"We've got to get her to the hospital. We have Narcan there."

"Will she be okay?"

"It depends on how quickly we get there and whether this drug responds."

Together they lifted Claire onto a stretcher. Seeing her limp, unresponsive like this… If Nate had been having a hard time earlier reconciling the adventurous Claire he'd known in college with this subdued version who was trying to seem happy with life in her small town, he was *really* having trouble with this picture. Claire had always seemed so full of life to him.

But no one was invincible. And if this really was the result of her being dosed with Wicked, then the drug lived up to its name. They carried her down the stairs, loaded her into the ambulance. Nate couldn't ride with her. He wasn't family, wasn't anything to her.

So why did he care more than it felt like he should if she was just a responsibility in this case?

Maybe because it was ultimately his fault she was like this right now. If he'd been quicker, if he'd trusted the right people during his last undercover op, hadn't been betrayed, they could have had the Carson brothers already in custody by now, could have used the leverage of evidence against them to catch the manufacturers of Wicked and stop the production of the drug that might be the one in her system now.

Yes. Nate was almost sure it was. Why would the men after her use anything else when they had unlimited access to Wicked?

He pulled his phone out again and made his way back upstairs and into Claire's house for a little more privacy. The police had arrived and were processing the scene, but they were a safer audience than he'd get if he had this conversation out on the street. He stood just inside the doorway so that he couldn't be easily overheard. "Wade?" he said when his boss answered the call to his direct line. "I need to know everything we know about the chemical composition of Wicked, how to counteract it. Can you send that to me immediately?"

"You've got it. Call me later and tell me what this is about."

Never more thankful for his boss's confidence in him, Nate downloaded the email that popped up on his phone moments later, ran down the stairs, climbed onto his bike and gunned the gas as hard as he could in the direction of the hospital.

SIX

By the time Nate had arrived at the hospital, they'd administered Narcan—a drug designed as an antidote to opiates—and Claire seemed to be responding to that. It turned out he hadn't needed to get that extra info on Wicked, but it had been all he could think to do at the time. He was thankful even a small town like Treasure Point had excellent medical professionals who knew what they were doing.

"She'll be asleep for a while," the doctor told Nate when he got there. "She's no longer sedated, but her body is exhausted."

"So she's not in a coma or anything?"

The doctor shook his head. "She should be fine. There's no indication that there will be any permanent damage. I'll be back to check later."

Nate stood there for a minute, then sank into a chair. Matt and Gemma had come to the hospital immediately after he had—he'd called them on his way over. They'd stepped out to find food but should be back any minute.

For now? He wasn't going to leave her alone.

Every beeping of every machine reminded Nate of how close Claire had been to dying. How close the drug trade had come to taking another life, this one truly innocent.

The hospital room was inevitably stark, even though they'd added the usual touches to try to make it homey—like the wallpaper border at the top of the wall. To celebrate the season, there was even a small wreath hanging on the door.

Nate had almost forgotten how fast Christmas was approaching.

Matt and Gemma came back and got reassurances from the nurse that Claire was improving, and then Matt told Gemma they needed to go home.

"But she's my sister," Nate heard her argue in an exhausted voice.

"Yes, and she's going to be staying at our house as soon as the hospital releases her. She needs you to be alert and able to take care of her."

With that, Gemma quit fighting, though it was plain to see she was still reluctant to go. Nate promised to stay and update them on her condition. If they wondered why he cared enough to stay—Nate wasn't under the impression that they knew he and Claire had been friends before—they didn't ask. And Nate didn't volunteer. He wasn't sure himself. Was their past friendship really the explanation? They hadn't kept in touch—he hadn't even thought about her in a long time before he'd discovered he was coming to Treasure Point, the home she had mentioned so many times. So why did he feel invested? He honestly wasn't sure. He just knew he'd done a lot of scary things in his life, but that none of them had scared him quite as much as seeing Claire on the floor like that.

"Coffee?" a nurse asked when she came in to check Claire's vitals. "You must be exhausted."

"I'd love some."

She left without another word, but when she came back, she surveyed him as she handed him the cup. "You must care about her a lot to be here."

"Oh, it's..." He stopped talking. He'd been about to tell her that it was nothing, that he wasn't in any kind of relationship with Claire. But then again... Wheels started to turn in his mind. "It's the least I could do," he finished. And that was the truth.

"I'm Jody Keller. I went to school with Claire. Everyone loves her. I hope you know how special she is. And treat her that way." With a look that was a combination of a friend warning a guy not to hurt her friend and a smile, she went on her way.

Nate took another sip of coffee, looking at Claire's face relaxed in sleep. After everything he'd seen yesterday, that look of peace on her face was about all he could ask for today.

Sometimes it was easy to lose sight of the details in his fight against drugs. It wasn't just about saving the world from their influence, from their danger. It was about individual people.

Melanie. Jenni. Claire.

It was too late for the first two. But not for Claire.

And Nate wasn't going to let anything happen to her.

He took another sip of coffee, mulling over the plan that had begun to form when the nurse assumed he and Claire were together.

She needed someone to look out for her until all of this was over—that was clear. Although the Treasure Point Police Department was now taking the threat against her seriously and had an officer stationed outside her door, Nate knew he wouldn't sleep in his hotel room without someone in the room with her, so he'd volunteered himself. That took care of tonight. But what would happen tomorrow?

He'd hashed out some details of her security with the chief while they were waiting for the doctor to stabilize her. It had seemed like the best thing to do—plan on her making it and come up with a strategy to make sure she *stayed* alive. The chief had told him that Officer O'Dell had volunteered to have her stay at his house—with her sister, who was O'Dell's wife. That way an officer could be with her at night, the hours that were usually hardest to protect someone. Clay Hitchcock, who had night patrol, would spend more time than usual surveying the area for threats.

Daytime, however, was still unaccounted for. The chief had no suggestions except the possibility of her staying at the police station all day. Claire would hate the idea of closing her coffee shop until this was over, but there was no way to make her shop fully secure. Even if an officer was stationed there with her, too many people were in and out, in direct contact with Claire at the register. Someone could attack her easily.

If it was necessary for her safety for her to stay at the station, then fine. But Nate had been chasing these guys for eighteen months. He couldn't promise they were going to resolve it all quickly, although he hoped for Claire's sake that they would. And cooping her up in the police station like she was a prisoner herself would be more and more cruel the longer it lasted.

What if Nate could stay with her during the day? It would benefit Claire because she'd have someone watching her back all the time, someone who was armed and knew how to use deadly force if it became necessary. And it would benefit Nate because he could investigate better, do more surveillance, with another person. Two people stood out in a crowd much less than a lone man. Hardly anyone would take note of Nate with his camera if he was accompanied by Claire. Especially since she was apparently well liked all over town, someone people admired and trusted. And what better cover for them to spend all their time together than to let the town think they had started dating?

It was the perfect solution all around. Now to get Claire to agree.

She shifted in the bed, and for a moment, he thought she might wake up. Nate bounced his leg, working out some of his nervousness at pitching his idea to her. He wished he had some idea of how she would respond, but as he'd realized yesterday, they weren't the same people who had been friends in college. The two of them really had been friends only because of their mutual connection with Justin. And given the way things had ended there, he couldn't blame Claire for wanting distance from Nate, too. Pretending to be a couple wouldn't be easy for her, even if it was the best way to keep her safe.

That plan was all they had.

Twenty minutes or so later, Nate had finished his coffee and Claire stirred again.

This time she opened her eyes.

"Nate?" She frowned a little. "Where am I?"

"The hospital."

She nodded. "That's right. I woke up earlier for a minute and figured that out. I guess I fell sleep again."

"Do you feel up to talking about what happened?"

Nate didn't know if it was better to wait, to give her more time to recover, but she looked good right now. The doctor had been by again to reassure him that she would be fine. Time wasn't a luxury they had on their side right now, so it seemed better to work on plans than not.

"I can talk. First, about what happened…"

Nate got up and shut the door. He doubted anyone was listening in the hospital, but it was better to be safe than sorry.

"You tasted dinner, didn't you?" Nate asked. This was the question he'd been waiting to ask her when she woke up. The spoon had been found on the floor.

"I did. And right after I felt…it felt like a big rush of adrenaline and then, just I was falling, though I managed to break the fall a little by grabbing hold of the counter. It happened too fast to call out to you or anything."

"The police went back to process the scene. Shiloh feels awful for not taking the spices as evidence the first time. From what everyone can tell, that's how you were poisoned, with the drug I've been investigating. Wicked."

"Nice name. It fits." Claire made a face. "Any more leads on who's behind this?"

"Not yet. I made a call to the GBI headquarters while you were sleeping. They're looking into known associates of the Carson brothers again so I can make sure there's no one I should be investigating in surrounding towns."

"Surrounding towns?" Her shoulders relaxed slightly. "So you don't think anyone from Treasure Point is connected to your case?"

Nate hesitated. "I don't know. I can't promise that one way or the other."

"I hope not."

"Why?"

Claire shrugged. "I'd hate to think that the person after me could be someone I know and consider a friend."

Of course she felt that way. Betrayal from those closest to you was the worst kind. Nate knew that well, knew it from when he'd misplaced his trust and almost brought the whole investigation crashing down around him and the others. When they'd barely escaped alive...

He needed to bring the conversation back to the point, push the screams of his coworkers as they'd been ambushed out of his mind.

As he struggled to form words, thankfully Claire spoke up. "So what the plan from here on out? Still the same as it was? Sleep at Matt and Gemma's and be careful at my shop during the day?"

Nate watched her expression closely, curious how she was going to respond. "Actually, I have a proposition for you."

"What's that?" Nate's facial expression gave very little away. Claire could tell that he was watching *her* closely, but that was it.

"You need protection twenty-four hours a day. That's pretty clear now."

"Okay."

"I talked to the chief—"

"*You* talked to the chief? Like it's your responsibility to figure out what to do with me?" Claire raised her eyebrows. "We might have been friends at one point, Nate, but you have no right—"

"Listen, let's not argue. The chief agrees with me, and

we've worked it out with Matt and Gemma for you to stay with them until this is over. That way Matt can be on protective duty at night, essentially, and Clay Hitchcock will also patrol that area heavily."

"What about during the day?"

"That's the problem so far. You can't be in the shop." She opened her mouth to protest. "And before you say anything, that's not coming from me. It's coming from the chief. A busy shop like yours is just too hard to secure."

Claire scowled as she tried to think of an argument and failed. Okay, so she'd have to close the shop until this was settled. It was aggravating, but ideally it wouldn't be for long.

"So what am I supposed to do all day? Just sit around Matt and Gemma's house?"

"No, that wouldn't really be safe, either," Nate pointed out. "Not when Matt's away on duty. The chief offered to let you stay in their conference room during the day." It was nice that they were taking her safety seriously… but the conference room?

She raised her eyebrows again. "If you have a better idea than that, I'm open to it."

"What would you think about spending time with me?"

Too many comebacks came to mind.

"In a work capacity," Nate finished, shaking his head and smiling a little. "You give away a lot with your facial expressions. Did you know that?"

She'd never been very good at disguising her emotions. "So we'd be together all day?"

"Yes."

"But you're supposed to be investigating. How's that going to work if you're on babysitting duty?"

"Actually, you would just come with me. I'm not in deep cover right now, so I'm not intentionally spending time around the criminals I'm tracking. This is more of a surveillance operation. Now that we have reason to believe there's someone else in charge of this operation, my assignment is to get the lay of the land—see if I can find any information to identify the man in charge or gather evidence we can use to make the Carson brothers try to make a deal with us. My orders are to keep my eyes open in general. I don't want to do anything too proactive right now to spook anyone. If you stay with me every day, that gives you protection from whoever's after you. It also helps me with my cover."

"But how would I be helping with that?"

"People are almost always more likely to notice a lone man than a couple."

"So…you don't just want me to be with you all the time. You want us to pretend to be dating? I'm not going to lie for you, Nate."

"I'm undercover, not a liar. I'm not asking you to do that."

"But you want to pretend…what?"

"We'll let people assume what they want. Most will assume we're together, yes. But that's not just better for my cover. It's better for you, too. And you don't have to lie to anyone. If someone asks, tell the truth—that we're old friends getting to know each other again."

She considered it. It certainly sounded more interesting than hanging around the police station all day. And if she could help him with his investigation, then they might be able to resolve things faster, meaning she wouldn't have to wait as long to get back to her regular life.

"So will you do it?"

"Do what?" Claire's eyes were wide. Innocent.

"Show me the town, go on some dates, see if it can put us one step closer to solving this case?"

Claire nodded. "It's not the most romantic proposition I've heard, but yeah. I'll do it."

Nate shook his head. Claire knew she was making light of the situation as a sort of coping mechanism, but she could tell from his face that Nate didn't blame her. The truth was that she didn't feel anywhere near this lighthearted, but in a situation like this, what else could she do? People had to find a way to bend under pressure this immense, or they broke.

Claire didn't want to break.

SEVEN

Claire watched as Nate climbed out of her little car and walked to her side—he'd still had the keys from when he'd driven her in it the other day and he'd driven it to the hospital to pick her up. Was he really… Yes, yes he was, she decided only once he'd reached for the door handle. He was opening her door for her.

"Didn't you turn into a gentleman?" she teased as she climbed out. She felt better today, more like herself.

"Just trying to make it believable," he teased back.

"Well, if we're going for believable…" She grinned up at him. "Shouldn't you hold my hand?" She reached it out, not believing she was doing this. Was she really offering Nate Torres her hand? Flirting with him a little?

He took her hand, and Claire knew immediately it had been a bad idea. She hadn't dated a man outside of a few disastrous first dates in years and had forgotten how much her hand safely wrapped in a man's could affect her.

And she'd done this to herself. Clearly Claire had lost her mind. That was really the only explanation she had to offer herself—and besides, didn't they say if you did the same thing and expected different results, that was the very definition of insanity?

How many times did she have to remind herself that Nate was *more* of a risk-taker than Justin? If the black leather and motorcycle hadn't told her, you'd think his choice of job would. Claire had given up anything that hinted at risk or danger after the accident. The one that had almost killed her. The one that *had* killed Justin.

The pressure on her hand increased, so fast she might have imagined it. Or Nate might have squeezed her hand. Claire took a deep breath, resisted the urge to pull away, knowing that her safety depended on having someone qualified to protect her around all the time. This charade with Nate allowed her so much more freedom than hiding in the police station.

She had to make this work. Had to sell it to anyone watching.

"You okay?"

"Yeah. Fine." She kept her words short, prayed they were true. She wanted them to be. Surely that counted.

"So we'll stick to the route we talked about earlier?"

"Sounds good to me. It's not just the closest to town. They're also the best lights. It's the route I take every time I go out."

"Every year, you mean?"

Claire laughed. "No, every time. I go at least three times a year to look at lights. There's something about the brightness in the middle of the winter darkness. I mean, I know everyone loves it, but I just can't get enough. I'm kind of a fan of Christmas." Understatement.

"I…" Nate drew out the word, hesitated, then finished

his thought, his voice lowering in tone and volume. "I haven't celebrated Christmas much in years."

"No Christmas?"

He shrugged. "I wouldn't say none at all. I acknowledge the day, thank God for the gift of His Son."

Nate was a Christian? She didn't remember him talking about it in college. Maybe it was recent?

"But you don't celebrate?"

"No."

The one-word response didn't invite conversation, but Claire had a sister who liked to keep details to herself, so she was used to prying things out of people.

"Want to tell me why?"

Nate didn't answer right away. They walked by a house decorated in all-white lights—Claire preferred colors—and still he said nothing. He didn't even seem to be looking at the lights but instead was looking around them—scanning for trouble, she would imagine—or occasionally down at his feet.

Maybe she should learn that pressing people for conversation wasn't always a good thing.

Claire was about to retract the question—well, as much as one could—when he finally spoke up.

"Christmas was my sister, Melanie's, favorite holiday."

He said it like it needed no further explanation, and for a minute Claire wasn't sure what to do. She'd just made a resolution not to pry so much, but...wasn't he inviting her to?

"And your sister...?" she prompted after several beats of silence had passed.

"She's gone."

Claire stopped walking. Let the words and the stillness and the cold soak into her.

"Gone?"

He nodded. "She died eight years ago, my senior year of college. Overdosed on drugs."

Senior year. Justin had graduated two years ahead of Claire. By the time she and Nate were in their senior year, everything had already ended. She'd lost touch with Nate…right when he probably could have used friends around the most.

Claire shivered, and not from the cold. If Melanie had died from drugs…that was why Nate put the effort he did into investigating drug-related crimes, why it meant more to him than just an abstract struggle of good versus evil. There was nothing abstract about that fight for him—it was real. True to life.

Of course she couldn't say any of that now. Not here in the middle of the street.

Instead she nodded, and wondered if it was her imagination that Nate seemed to be walking a little closer to her.

Claire had taken his story about his sister and tucked it somewhere inside her heart, it seemed. She'd asked a few questions, but not many. She hadn't changed how she treated him, hadn't overdone the pity, but he could tell she cared.

Felt his hurt with him.

Nate wasn't used to that reaction, hadn't been prepared for it. He wasn't sure, but he thought he might have pulled Claire toward him as they'd talked. And… it had nothing to do with his cover.

Everything to do with wanting her close.

And it was completely inappropriate. He put more distance between them. Sharing what he had about his sister, something she hadn't known even though it had happened just after they'd lost touch, was bound to make him feel close to her somehow. That didn't mean anything. All of that, plus his past friendship with Claire—when she'd always fascinated him but had been off-limits because she'd been dating his best friend—was irrelevant. This was a case. She was in danger. He was protecting her. And that was all.

"Are you cold?" he asked her, needing something to say to change the subject, something to uncharge the air around them.

Claire shook her head. "No, I'm okay. Besides, even if I was, looking at Christmas lights is worth it."

Maybe it was. Seeing it through Claire's eyes…he could understand the special kind of holiday excitement in the tiny twinkle lights on the houses in town that made people like Claire love celebrating the holiday. The decorations were bright in the dark, like little bits of hope.

Maybe that was what his Christmases had been missing. Every holiday, every *day* since his sister had died was tinged with a hint of defeat, like evil had won. Even though Nate knew it wasn't true…that fact didn't do much to change how he felt, especially around days like Christmas.

Claire pointed to some lights on their right, giving him a welcome interruption from his thoughts. "That's where I used to live."

The house was a cute Southern cottage-style house, exactly the kind of place where he could picture this new version of Claire living.

"Do you miss it?"

"No. It makes more sense for me to live above the shop right now. But maybe someday I'll have a place like it again."

"You want to stay in Treasure Point, then."

From what he'd seen over the past few weeks, how much the town loved her, how different she was from how she'd been in college, Nate hadn't expected her to hesitate, but she did.

"Yes. I do want to stay."

"You do?"

"What? Is that so bad, staying in a small town forever?" Her sweet voice had changed to carry a hint of indignation, and she dropped his hand.

"No, I just—"

But she interrupted him. "Because you don't know everything about me, okay? You think you've got some things figured out after being a part of my life a decade ago, but you don't. What you see is what you get now, a small-town girl with no dreams of living anywhere else. Not anymore."

"Okay." He held his hands up in mock surrender and blew out a breath. "I didn't mean to turn this into an argument. You hesitated, Claire, when I said something about you staying here. I just wondered what that meant."

She'd said *not anymore*. What had changed? Claire, obviously. But what had changed *her*?

The next house had an impressive lights display, too, and Claire seemed to forget she'd been upset. They continued down that street, and another, and Nate wondered if there was any town with more Christmas spirit than this one. He hadn't seen this many Christmas lights in one place since he was a kid.

The only thing bothering Nate was that he felt he should have been able to relax. Instead the opposite seemed to be happening—with every step he got a little tenser. Until he started to feel like someone was watching them.

And it was too distinct a feeling, too familiar, for him to ignore.

"I think it's about time to head back." He'd thought about phrasing it as a question, but he didn't really want to give Claire an option. He'd ignored warning signals like this before, and it had never ended well. He wasn't going to take any chances.

They walked together, but without saying anything, for the rest of the short distance to town. Nate held his breath a little as they walked in the darkest spot of their stroll so far—a section between the neighborhood and downtown where streetlights didn't reach well. Should he tell Claire to hurry through it? Tell her that he'd been feeling like someone was tracking them?

No. Better not to worry her when it might be nothing. He was enjoying seeing Claire more relaxed. He'd had a couple of weeks to observe her in her shop before everything had changed, and while she'd seemed happy enough running her coffee shop, she'd also seemed tense. She was wound up tight there, a perfectionist.

That wasn't the way she'd been the time that he, Justin, Katie and Claire had driven up to North Georgia and gone hang gliding. It was like there were two different versions of her. Nate thought the girl he'd known in college, the risk-taker, was the real Claire. She'd certainly seemed happier and freer. But then again, he couldn't say for sure, and maybe it wasn't his business. They certainly weren't good enough friends now for him to pry.

They made it through the dark stretch of road without incident. They stepped back into the orange glow of the downtown streetlights, and Nate exhaled in relief. Maybe he was off his game and overly watchful.

And then shots split the air.

Claire's scream drowned out everything except the next two shots, which came even closer to hitting them.

"Run!" he yelled to Claire. The loud decibel level of the shots told Nate that it was a rifle shooting at them. That meant that their would-be killer could have been anywhere.

Nate followed Claire as she dashed across the street, down a sidewalk, past several open storefronts that would have made good places to take cover, into her own coffee shop.

"Are you crazy?" he yelled as glass rained from one of the front windows.

"Crazy? Why? Here, behind the counter." She dove behind it and Nate followed.

She was at the edge, positioned so she could look around. "Move!" he ordered. She scooted further in but scowled at him.

"I wanted to be able to see," she said.

She wanted to see the bullets flying at them? Sure. Except no. Nate shook his head, decided they'd talk more about it later.

"I've got an actual weapon I can use to defend us if I need to. I think that along with my training makes it a better idea that I be here."

"But if you shoot back," Claire's voice broke into Nate's thoughts just as his hand was moving for his weapon, "won't they know you're undercover?"

He hesitated. Here in Georgia? Probably not. Concealed carry was common enough. It wasn't like he was going to flash his badge at anyone. But there was still the risk…

It didn't matter. If he got a clear shot, he would take it. Claire's life was worth more than this investigation.

"Call the police, Claire."

He heard her moving around behind him, immediately doing as he'd asked. Her voice didn't even waver as she explained the situation, and she even managed to be vague on whom she was with. Hadn't gotten flustered in the pressure and said, "I'm with an undercover GBI agent."

The gunshots had stopped well before they'd taken cover. He thought back. There had been the initial shot, then two more almost right after. One more when they'd entered the shop, shattering the front window. Only four shots total. Nate's tension didn't ease but grew. What were the chances that whoever had been shooting at them was changing positions, moving closer to them now for an ambush?

"How did this happen? How did they know exactly where you'd be?"

"I think that may be my fault," Claire confessed. "I let it slip in the hospital cafeteria that you and I were going to look at Christmas lights. I was just telling Matt and Gemma when we were there for lunch, but I thought if anyone overheard, that it would be good, that it would help build our covers."

He understood the logic. Unfortunately it had backfired badly.

At least the threat seemed to be over for the moment, though they'd lay low just in case. Nate didn't see anything in the streetlight-lit darkness beyond the dim shop. Not until he saw a Treasure Point cruiser pull up with its lights flashing. Officer Matt O'Dell climbed out of the car.

He strode inside with even more purpose than another officer would have.

"Are you okay, Claire?" he asked as soon as he was inside the shop. "Where are you?"

"Behind the counter. With Nate."

He appreciated the way she'd reminded the man that he was there. It was never a good idea to surprise officers with more people than they were expecting.

O'Dell came behind the counter, went straight for Claire. "You're okay?" He stared her down. "Honest?"

"Yes." The word came out surprisingly steady.

"Come on. I'll take you back to the house. Several officers are on their way, and they can handle the scene."

Claire didn't insist on staying. But she didn't fall apart, either. Something that made Nate think she had more of a brave spirit still in her than she realized.

As soon as the other officers arrived, Matt saw to it that Claire was safely inside her car.

"I'll meet you back here tomorrow, okay?" Nate confirmed before she shut the door. She agreed, and then drove off, followed closely by Matt's cruiser. He stood outside for a minute, the cold air and the memories of what had just happened chilling him.

He looked around, trying to determine where the shots had come from. Possibly from another shop on the street? But Nate thought it was more likely that someone had been waiting on the rooftop across the street from Kite Tails and Coffee. That vantage point gave them the most advantage, both to shoot at them as they approached downtown, and to follow up if necessary right at Claire's front door.

What amazed Nate was the lengths someone was going to make sure Claire was dead. Why was she such a threat? Just because of the painting? Or maybe there was something she might have overheard at her shop? He couldn't be sure of anything other than that Claire was in a lot of danger. Unfortunately, no matter what Nate did, until they caught whoever was giving the orders in this particular smuggling ring, there was little they could do to stop the possibility of more attacks. All they could do was try to protect Claire from the would-be killer.

He walked back into the coffee shop.

"Rifle," Shiloh confirmed as she dug a bullet out of one of Claire's cabinets. "It's what I expected, but it's good to confirm."

"I'm assuming that the weapon used at Jenni's murder wasn't a rifle." Most close-range, one-on-one crimes like that involved handguns.

"You're right. It was a .38 caliber revolver. We just got ballistics back on it today."

"And what do you think?"

Shiloh shook her head. "I know it's more complicated than it looks, but Johnson has a .38 that has been fired recently. That and the positive residue test for Trace makes that part of it look pretty straightforward. I'm almost sure he pulled the trigger."

"But was he acting on orders, because of his ties to the Carsons? Or is he the one who wanted Jenni dead?"

"That's the question I'm still trying to answer."

Nate nodded. "I'll let you guys work. I'm going to head back to the hotel to check in with the boss." A quick phone call would let him update Wade on what had happened.

"Get some sleep. This doesn't seem to be slowing down anytime soon."

Nate nodded his agreement, then walked out into the darkness, started toward the hotel and gazed at the town, all decorated for Christmas.

The town looked safe, harmless, like it didn't hold a single secret. But the truth was that around any given corner, someone from a drug ring intent on seeing Claire dead could be hiding.

The truth was, appearances were deceiving.

EIGHT

By the time Claire—accompanied by Matt, who had followed her there in his own car—arrived at the coffee shop the next morning to survey the damage, Nate was there already, sitting on the sidewalk, leaning against the side of the building with his eyes closed.

"Waiting for somebody?" she asked, and his eyes opened. She waved at Matt as he drove away. Slowly. It had been a pretty difficult job to convince him to stick to the original plan of having Nate be in charge of her security during the day, but realistically, there was nothing else that could be done. Sure, today was Matt's day off, but the rest of the time he had his own assignments elsewhere in town. Nate was the best option for keeping her safe.

"I was awake."

Claire raised her eyebrows. "Sure. Want a cup of coffee?"

"You're okay with going back in, after yesterday? We don't have to, if you'd rather not."

She laughed. Surely the man realized that after being almost abducted a few days ago, then having her house broken into, then being shot at, she wasn't very easily intimidated. If she got scared of every place she'd been attacked, then she wouldn't feel safe anywhere in town.

"I'm fine." Last night had shaken her up more than she wanted to admit. She'd had no trouble being honest with Gemma and Matt about how scared she'd been. But Nate was a different story. He'd been there for some of the bravest moments of her life. She couldn't handle the thought of him being thoroughly disappointed in her inability to handle some danger.

Although in fairness, someone wanting her dead was more danger than she'd ever faced, even on her most risk-loving days.

"I'll take that coffee, then," Nate said.

"I figured as much. Do we have plans for today? I thought you might keep me company while I clean up inside the shop."

"Sure. That works."

Claire unlocked the door—a sad kind of precaution, locking it at all, when the front window was boarded and taped closed. She smiled. The police officers last night must have completed the makeshift repair to discourage people from entering. Still, Claire knew that anyone who wanted to get into the shop could easily do so. "I think I'm going to take my paintings down and put them in storage somewhere for the time being." It was more of a thought, something she hadn't meant to say out loud.

"I think that's a good idea." Nate's reply confirmed that she had spoken it aloud. Oh well.

She entered the shop, Nate following closely on her heels. Claire shivered in the air—slightly cooler than the outside—and wondered if she should have let him go inside first. Surely no one was lurking in the darkness, waiting to kill her now…were they?

Why shouldn't they be? Someone wanted her dead enough to try to take a sniper-style shot at her in the middle of downtown. Nothing should have surprised her at this point.

Nate's hand on her arm startled her. She turned, finding his face closer than she'd expected, their eyes meeting immediately. Claire turned away.

"I, uh…" Nate cleared his throat. "I'd rather go first and check things out if you don't mind."

She nodded. "Of course. Thank you." That would give her a minute to control whatever crazy emotions were bubbling inside her, probably fear that had gotten misplaced into a buzzy feeling.

Claire stepped aside as Nate passed, keeping her back to the wall. After standing there for a minute, watching as Nate checked the shop over to make sure it was empty, she slid into a booth, rested her head on her hand.

Almost started truly to process the danger of her situation—to let everything that had happened in the last few days sink in. But what good would come of that? It would just make her more scared when it already took everything she had just to hold herself together.

So she stood up, found a broom and started to sweep. She wasn't ready for anything more than that yet. "Finding anything?" she asked Nate, keeping her voice lighter than her spirits felt.

"Nothing. It's all clear."

No visible threat. Claire wanted to let that fact give her some reassurance, calm the tension she could feel building in her shoulders. But every time so far that she'd almost lost her life, there had been no sign of danger beforehand.

At least…she didn't think so.

"Nate?"

"Yeah?"

"Can we talk?" Claire put the broom down and moved toward where she'd heard his voice, far in the back.

"Sure, just give me a minute," he replied. He was in the storage room, checking behind a couple more shelves. She was thankful for his help. She grabbed an unopened—couldn't be too careful after that poisoning incident—pound of coffee from the shelf and moved to the coffeemaker to put coffee on for them.

"You wanted to talk?" he asked her a few minutes later.

She turned to face him, looking him straight in the eyes. She was ready for an answer, even though in the last five or ten minutes she'd all but decided that she knew what it was. The only positive was that it made her too angry to remember to be scared.

"Did you know?"

"Know what?"

Here she went again, not speaking clearly when she was frustrated. Claire let out a breath. "Did you know," she started again, slowly this time, each word deliberate, "that I was in danger yesterday before the shots started flying?"

Nate didn't answer for a minute. The set of his mouth didn't change. His face was like a mask she hadn't learned how to look past yet.

"We had talked about this earlier last night, Claire. You knew that you were in danger. So I'm not entirely sure that I know what you're asking."

"In the moments before." Claire poured the coffee, grateful to have something to do with her hands. "Did you recognize that we were in more danger than we had been? Did you know we were about to be attacked? Were there signs I missed? Or were you as blindsided as I was?"

His expression shifted, just for a second, but enough that Claire knew she had her answer. It was like someone had punched her in the stomach, stealing the breath from her lungs.

Nate had known. The man she'd trusted with her life had known something was about to happen and had kept silent rather than trusting her with the truth.

Her head and heart debated what she should do for a second. Run? Find somewhere to think through this without his handsome, possibly dishonest face so close to her?

It just hurt so much to think that Nate hadn't trusted her, hadn't believed she could handle knowing what was really going on. Her family tended to underestimate her ability to handle a crisis. Gemma was the sister who'd been through the fire and come out stronger. Claire… she was the sweet one. No one wanted to risk upsetting her. Was Nate doing the same thing her family did? Because if he was, that choice could have far greater consequences for her than a little stung pride. Her life was at risk. She needed to know when she was in active danger if she was going to do anything to help keep herself alive.

Though she and Nate hadn't been friends in years, she'd thought he'd have more confidence on her. See her as tough even though the rest of Treasure Point surely didn't. The town had a role for her to play, and she played it well. But she wasn't the sweet girl next door who was too weak to handle life that they thought she was. She was almost thirty, had seen enough of life to know that it wasn't perfect, it wasn't predictable. Oh, she knew that too well...

Yet she tried her best to keep her life looking just that way. Perfect and predictable. Because the town expected it, or because it felt safer to her? Claire honestly didn't know.

So this time Claire didn't run. Instead she faced him directly, lifted her chin a little. "I am not a child."

"Never meant to treat you like one."

"But you are, Nate. I need protection, sure. I'm not stupid enough to think I can fully handle this...situation on my own. It's over my pay grade, drug dealers and murderers." Claire shook her head, still not quite believing the words she could hear coming out of her own mouth.

"Which is why I didn't see any need to alarm you when we were looking at Christmas lights. Yeah, I'd started to feel like we were being watched, but I had no proof, just gut instinct, which has been wrong before. We had to get to cover. We had to walk that way. You agreed to head back this way. It wasn't like I had to convince you. We were already doing the appropriate thing. There was no reason for me to tell you I was getting more concerned when there was literally nothing you could do about it!"

"But I would have known."

"And if anything, that could have put you in more danger. I don't need some crazy heroics out of you in a situation like that that you aren't trained to handle. I need you to stay back and let me handle it."

Claire glared at him, hating the fact that every word he said made sense.

"That's why I didn't say anything. Believe me, Claire,

if I'd seen a sniper, I would have said something to you so I could get you to a covered position as quickly as possible."

Slight consolation, at least.

Claire hesitated, debated whether or not she was done. "One more thing." She swallowed hard, willing her racing heart to settle down. "I know this arrangement is mostly for my protection, and a little bit for your cover. But I know this town, I know these people, and I think I can actually help you with your investigation, if you're willing to let me. I'm asking you to. Please, let me."

Nate opened his mouth to reply but never got the chance to answer. A cluster of screams and shouts came from somewhere outside the shop. Nate was the first to react—of course—and headed straight for the door.

"You stay here," he called over his shoulder as he took off in the direction of the noise.

Like she was really going to listen to that. Hadn't they just had this conversation? She wasn't charging into danger like an action movie hero, but she would see what was going on—maybe spot something that Nate might miss, something only a local would notice.

Claire did pause for a second, made sure she didn't see anyone or anything that looked threatening, and then took off after him toward the docks.

The body that had washed up onto the grassy patch of sand not far from the Treasure Point dock was in no shape to be recognized—exposure to ocean creatures and salt water had taken care of that. But Nate could tell one thing by looking at the exposed section of bone on the body's forehead.

Cause of death was likely a bullet to the head. Execution-style.

Nate kept calm as he waited for the Treasure Point police to get there, doing his best to make sure no one touched the body, while only looking like a take-charge bystander.

Several officers he didn't recognize had just approached when Nate started to question his decision to run down here in the first place.

A body appeared on the beach the day after Claire was attacked again? What was to say this wasn't some sort of trap to lure him outside, leaving her unprotected? And if it was, he'd played right into it...

Nate wanted to watch the officers investigate. But more than that, he wanted to know Claire was safe. He hesitated only one more second, then turned and walked quickly back in the direction of her shop. He'd check in with her, get her somewhere safe—maybe her brother-in-law was off work and could protect her?—and then get back down to the docks. See what he could find out.

That decided, he walked with even more purpose. She'd be okay. She had to be. He'd find her in the shop, and she'd laugh at him...

Nate reached for the door, pulled it open.

The shop was empty. "Claire?" he called anyway though he didn't see or hear evidence of anyone still inside. He swallowed back a lump in his throat, and fear started to claw from the place inside him that had sprung into being as soon as he'd heard that his sister had died. The part of him that said he was never going to be able to stop people he cared about from getting hurt.

He moved through the shop, expecting the worst. But it was empty. No sign of her yet. Had she been grabbed?

Dragged away? Heart pounding uncomfortably, he hurried back to the door, pushed it open and turned left toward the docks.

He ran straight into Claire, her surprised expression and her presence registering too late for him to do anything to stop himself from slamming into her. She stumbled back, but Nate did manage to reach out and steady her.

"Nate! What—?"

But Claire didn't finish what she was saying, because once he'd reached for her arms and steadied her, saw she was *alive* and fine, he couldn't quite make himself let go. Instead he pulled her closer, wrapped his arms around her.

For about a second and a half, he felt… Nate wasn't even sure. His mind wouldn't let him settle on one feeling. All he really knew was that for that second and a half, having his arms around Claire Phillips felt like the most right thing in the world.

And then she pulled away, just slightly, but enough to make him wonder what in the world he was doing. He dropped his arms like she'd burned him. And good thing—because any longer and she probably would have.

Nate had no business holding her at all, not when they could never have a relationship. And they couldn't—he couldn't put a woman through a job like his. Relationships couldn't handle that kind of stress. He'd watched countless law enforcement officers he'd worked with struggle through their crumbling marriages. Nate hadn't meant to start anything with that hug. It had just been a reaction to seeing her safe. He hadn't planned to feel anything.

And now he knew he'd been naive to think he was

completely immune to Claire. He'd been attracted to her in college, but she'd been his friend's girlfriend then. Firmly off-limits. He needed to remind himself that even though she was single, she was still off-limits, at least for him. No room for negotiation.

"Let's go inside," he said to Claire before she could say anything in response to his out-of-the-blue embrace.

"What's up, Nate?" Claire asked in her calm voice, the one that made him feel like maybe she was the one helping him out instead of the other way around. Something about her soft Southern accent always felt like a shot of calm to his always-ready-to-fight nerves.

How was he supposed to explain what had gotten into him? Nate shoved a hand through his hair—a habit he'd worked hard to break, but that returned now and then just to irritate him. "I was worried about you, okay?"

"Because of what happened at the docks?"

Nate squeezed his eyes shut, the body still clear in his mind as though it were right in front of him. *Please, don't let her have seen that,* he prayed almost without thinking. Instinctively. The idea that Claire might have to deal with evil like that…

"I saw the body, Nate."

Her voice was quieter now, but not weak. He opened his eyes, slowly brought them up to meet hers.

She met his gaze unflinchingly. "Why would someone do that to another person?"

Nate shook his head. "Why would someone try to kill a coffee shop owner and artist who might have innocently seen something she shouldn't have? People are greedy and cruel, Claire."

"Do you know who it was?"

"No."

"Someone from the case?"

"Yes." He didn't even hesitate. She deserved the truth, even what little bits of it he was sure of.

"Why do you think so?"

"Gunshot wound to his head looks like a drug execution to me, and given the fact that we're in the middle of a drug investigation…it's connected. I just don't know how yet."

"When will you?"

"When I get an ID on that body. Any chance you think your brother-in-law might be willing to pass on that information?"

"It's his day off. Let me see if he and Gemma might want to have us over for breakfast. If we keep it social, we'll get information, and you'll keep your cover." His jaw must have dropped, because she was grinning at him. How did she think of these things with no law enforcement background?

"It sounds perfect."

Claire pulled out her phone and started texting. Five minutes and several chirps indicating returned messages later, and she looked back up at him. "Let's go have breakfast."

"Where's their house?"

"On the edge of town, near the marsh. Too far to walk. Mind if we take my car?" she asked before he could offer.

"You don't want a ride on my motorcycle?"

"Do I look like a motorcycle kind of girl to you?" She raised her eyebrows.

He opened his mouth to remind her of the times she'd ridden on the back of a motorcycle in college. But she cut him off. "Not did I *used to*. Do I *now*?" She didn't wait for an answer. "Come on, let's go."

They walked outside and down the sidewalk to Claire's car.

"You can actually drive again if you want." Claire tossed him the keys. "I'd rather ride most of the time."

He wasn't going to turn that down. He liked being in control too much to sit in the passenger seat if he could avoid it. "Thanks."

Though he'd told himself earlier that he was smart enough not to make the same mistake twice, Nate still had to use all of his focus to keep his eyes on the road and not let them drift to Claire. The way she'd handled today...

The thing about Claire was that with every crisis she seemed stronger. More capable. Somehow the testing of her mettle was proving her to be made of more solid stuff than Nate ever would have guessed.

And as the hug had reminded him earlier, he was having to fight harder than ever to keep thinking about her in only a professional light.

NINE

When Matt and Gemma's house came into view, Claire let out a deep breath she hadn't known she'd been holding. She was doing her best to be brave, to take the new developments in the case in stride and not fall apart, but she could feel herself fraying around the edges. She hoped talking to her sister would help. *Gemma* was genuinely strong. Lately Claire felt like she wasn't—but she wanted to be.

"We're here," she confirmed for Nate in case he'd taken in the cypress cabin on stilts and decided she'd given him the wrong directions on accident. From the outside, it just looked like some old fishing shack, but the inside was gorgeous and homey.

"Claire, listen," Nate said before she could get out of the car, "...about that hug earlier. I was out of line. I freaked out a little when I couldn't find you, and I had just seen proof of what whoever's after you is capable of, but I shouldn't have—"

"Don't worry about it." She waved her hand, like she could wave off the memory of his touch so easily. Yeah, right. At least they both knew it shouldn't have happened and it meant nothing.

Claire looked away from Nate before he had a chance to say anything else, and she climbed out of the car. Talking to her sister was exactly what she needed. Not another second looking into his dark eyes.

"I'm glad you came, Claire!" Gemma called from the front porch while Claire was still making her way in that direction. Her sister pulled her into a hug as soon as she was close enough and squeezed her even tighter than usual. "You're okay?"

"Yes."

"Handling things okay?" Gemma looked her over when she asked this one, and Claire grappled with the right answer.

"I think so?"

Gemma shook her head. "You're going to have to do more than think so. Weathering things like this is half a mental battle."

"And the other half is managing not to get shot when my guard's down."

"So don't let your guard down. Ever," Nate said from behind her, sticking his hand out, around Claire, to shake Gemma's. "Thanks for having us this morning on such short notice."

"That's what family's for. And anyone who's a friend of Claire's gets the same welcome."

Would Claire consider Nate a friend, still? In college, yes. But now? They barely knew each other. Claire didn't know if she wanted them to be friends or not.

"So what do you want?" Nate asked, and Claire blinked. She was almost certain she hadn't spoken aloud, and if she had, she was going to find a rock to crawl under right now and never come out.

"Food first, or Matt's update?" he said slowly like

he was repeating it. "Which do you want to do first? If you're starving, I'd hate to make you wait."

"Food. Definitely."

They headed into the house, much to Claire's relief. She knew, at least in theory, that Nate was going to do his best to make sure she didn't get killed, but realistically, he couldn't predict everything or protect her from it. And out here, Claire didn't feel safe. She could see so many locations that could easily hide a sniper. This strip of land between the woods and the marsh was beautiful, but dangerous too—like so many things in life.

Not a thought she wanted to consider at the moment.

She followed her sister into the house, happy to know that Nate was behind her, keeping her safe from that direction.

Matt was in the kitchen making pancakes.

"You need any help?" Nate asked.

Claire turned around, raised her eyebrows. "You cook?"

He shrugged. "I can do okay."

"Sure," Matt answered, "you can come do the bacon."

"Want my help?" Claire felt like she should offer.

It was Nate who practically shooed her out of the kitchen. But Gemma seemed only too glad to get her alone. "You can help me fold laundry. I have a load of towels that just came out of the dryer."

Claire laughed but agreed. Gemma hated laundry.

"So what's up with Nate?" Gemma asked as soon as they were alone.

"What do you mean?"

"Just the way he's acting."

"What way?" Claire asked, frowning when Gemma

rolled her eyes. "No, I mean it. What way are you talking about? He's not doing anything unusual."

"The way he sticks to you like glue?"

"He's in charge of protecting me during the day."

"The way he's so nice to your sister and brother-in-law?"

"He's a nice guy."

"The way I kept catching him looking at you this morning when you're not paying attention? He seems like he knows you, Claire. Like he really sees you. Want to tell me why that is?"

But Claire wasn't ready to tell Gemma everything her sister didn't know about her past, wasn't ready to fill in the gaps. So instead she shrugged. "We've gotten to be friends," she said, which was the truth. Mostly.

Gemma stopped folding laundry, just looked at her for a minute. "Okay. I still think there's more to it, but if that's all you want to tell me, I guess I have to respect that."

The sisters talked a little more as they finished folding the laundry, before finally going to see if the men were done fixing breakfast. But the entire time, Claire could feel the distance between her and Gemma. She hated knowing she'd put it there. But she just wasn't ready to talk about the past.

That was one nice thing about Nate. He knew it all already. So with Nate, she didn't have to pretend.

"So, can you really cook or did you just want to talk without Gemma and Claire listening?" Matt looked up from the pancakes he was whisking to ask.

Nate laughed. "I can handle bacon, but yes, I did want to talk alone. What do you know about the body?"

"The one from the beach today?" He shook his head. "Sorry, we haven't heard anything about that one. I'll call you as soon as the ME gives us a positive ID."

Nate had tried not to speculate on whether the body was someone they knew was involved in the drug trade or if it was a new player. Or, for that matter, someone like Claire who'd just been in the wrong place at the wrong time. Who'd seen too much. That idea churned his stomach. It was a reminder of how badly someone wanted Claire dead. Drugs cost so many people their lives, good people *and* bad, but no matter what, all human life was valuable. He hated to see anyone's ended by this kind of evil.

"I'd appreciate that," Nate finally said.

"You have any idea who it might be?"

"No."

"But you think it's tied to your case."

"I'm hoping it is, because I'm hoping it will give us another lead to follow up on."

"The one thing we've found out so far is that the gunshot wound to our John Doe is the same caliber as the gun that killed Jenni."

"Really?"

"The ballistics report will tell us whether or not it was the same gun or not. But even now it looks likely that Jenni's death might have been a targeted hit rather than a crime of passion," Matt said.

"If our corpse is someone related to your case, yes."

"What other motive could a guy like Trace have for killing anyone besides his ex-girlfriend?"

"You're right. He's a scumbag, and though we knew he had ties to the Carson gang, we didn't believe he was very far into it. He's a weasel, but he's not the kind of scumbag I can picture killing multiple people. Looks like I could have been wrong."

"So *if* he was responsible… That puts time of death at least before Jenni's murder, because he's been in jail since then. Makes sense—I saw the body and it has definitely been in the water for several days, minimum."

"Yes," Nate said.

"Which means that even if he's involved, he's not the one who's trying to kill Claire."

"Exactly."

"So she's still in danger. You need to step back and let me handle it, don't you think?" Nate didn't know what to make of the way Matt was looking at him. If he hadn't known better, he would have said the man was trying to provoke him on purpose, start some kind of fight.

"I don't think that's a good idea. You can't keep her with you when you work during the day. What, you're going to leave her here with Gemma? You think that's safer than her being with me?" Nate shook his head. "Gemma's not trained. I'm not saying she's not tough, because I've heard bits and pieces about what she's been through in the past. But she can't keep Claire safe like I can."

"You sound very committed—but why? Just because you care about this case? Or because you want to be personally responsible for Claire's safety? I'm her brother-in-law. I have to ask. Besides, I just found out that the two of you were friends back when Claire was in college."

"This is a case for me. Nothing beyond that. Our past friendship is exactly that. Past."

Matt looked at him for a minute more. Nate held his gaze, feeling his face heat a little at his determination to be taken seriously. Finally the other man broke his gaze first. Looked down at the cast-iron pan in front of Nate.

"Speaking of paying attention and being careful… you're about to burn the bacon."

Nate moved the pan away before it could finish blackening. As it was it was…crispy. It would be fine.

"Do me a favor?" Matt said, his voice a little lower, more serious. "Be more careful with my wife's sister."

It was difficult to sit down in the chair next to Nate and pretend she hadn't heard part of his conversation in the kitchen. Difficult to meet her brother-in-law's eyes when she knew he'd heard Nate's words about how little she meant to him.

Not that they should upset her. *"This is a case for me. Nothing beyond that. Our past friendship is exactly that. Past."* It was exactly what he should have said. What she should feel.

But somehow…it wasn't what she felt at all. She was strong enough to not go there—she knew they weren't right for each other. But she was finally starting to admit that attraction to him was something she had to battle. So it hurt somehow to know that he wasn't having any of the same problems. That it was one-sided.

She needed to let it go, though, at least for now.

Gemma poured everyone coffee, Matt set a huge stack of pancakes onto the table and Nate brought in the bacon—which looked a tad charred around the edges to Claire. Finally everyone sat down.

"Nate, would you pray?"

If she wasn't imagining things, Matt had put Nate on the spot on purpose to gauge where he was spiritually. No doubt if he wasn't a Christian, he'd refuse. What she didn't know was why it mattered. Nate didn't need to be a believer to protect her—it would matter only if they had a deeper relationship, and hadn't Matt heard the complete brush-off Nate had given him about Claire in the kitchen?

"Sure."

Claire bowed her head, heartbeat quickening just a bit as they all reached for each other's hands and hers was back in Nate's. She didn't remember feeling quite this many *feelings* toward Nate when she and Justin were together. There had been attraction, sure. But…something about Nate and the way it felt to have any contact with him made Claire think they were one spark away from something more than friendship developing.

Focus on the prayer, she told herself.

It was over quickly, and she moved her hand out of his as fast as she could without seeming overeager.

"So, do we know anything new about the case?" Claire asked Matt, since she hadn't had a chance to talk to him so far.

"Not much."

The men glanced at each other.

"Okay, we can see the looks you're giving each other." Gemma laughed. "Care to explain?"

Matt pointed at his mouth—full of pancakes—and shrugged.

"Nothing where knowing the specifics would help you, Claire," Nate spoke up. "Only that we still don't know exactly who's after you."

Somehow she'd hoped progress had been made. She'd said several times that she knew the case wouldn't go terribly fast, but in truth she was growing impatient. She was ready to have her normal, predictable life back.

Of course, when she had that, Nate would be out of it...and oddly, she would miss him. But still, it was for the best. The sooner the better.

TEN

After breakfast, Nate had spent the day at the O'Dells' house. Gemma and Claire had roped the two men into playing a game, and then, when they'd gone off to another part of the house to do something else, Matt had taken Nate outside to show him his kayaks. Nate hadn't been surprised that he had some—with a location like this on the coast, it made sense that he'd have all kinds of boats. What had surprised him was that Matt made them himself. Nate had run his hand along one, feeling the impossibly smooth wood, and been impressed.

When late afternoon rolled around, Nate had confirmed that Matt would stay in the house with Claire, and that he'd see her again tomorrow, and then left. Nate's plan for the night was to grab some dinner at a little restaurant downtown and then go back to his hotel room. Before he'd left, Matt had given him a printout showing the locations of the boat slips in town and information about who was renting each of them.

It wasn't a promising lead, but he didn't have much to follow up on at the moment. Just knowing who was renting each of those slips could come in handy since most of the crimes had taken place in close proximity to the dock. Or it could be a waste of time, but he had to try. He didn't expect answers to these crimes to come too easily, but maybe something in that information could at least point him in the right direction. So far in his time doing surveillance around town he hadn't discovered much, but a break had to come sooner or later. For Claire's sake, he hoped it was sooner.

The Diner by the Sea—the actual name of the place, which he hadn't believed the first time he'd seen it—was a typical diner crossed with a beach restaurant. Faded carpet on the floor, but with tiny granules of sand in places. Clean, heavy tables, with brightly colored chairs. Crazy artwork that Nate supposed someone into modern art might have admired—but it was random to him, not something he could understand at all. In his opinion, Claire's art would have looked better. She was obviously talented even to someone like him who didn't know much about what was good or not, and what she painted made sense. It was reality, exactly as Claire saw it.

The sign told visitors to seat themselves, so Nate made his way to a table toward the corner. The very corner table was occupied already, which suited him fine. He liked to blend in, and the person at that table rarely did.

He opened his menu, scanning the choices before settling on chicken-fried steak. He set the menu down and waited. Apparently the service wasn't exactly known for its speed here.

While he waited, he looked around the room. The last time he'd come here had been at lunchtime, and there appeared to be a completely different crowd at dinner. Nate glanced at his watch. Seven o'clock. He'd guess that the demographics of the crowd were even varied from five until just a little later than now.

The waitress came—eventually—and then his food arrived. It was good, as good as food eaten alone could be. After he'd finished, Nate ordered coffee, planning to stick around a little longer in the hopes of overhearing something useful. In a small town like this, the discovery of the body was all anyone was talking about. He hoped that maybe people had noticed something—perhaps they recognized the man or had a theory as to who might be responsible. He'd listened carefully, but nothing helpful had come his way so far.

His coffee was down to the very bottom when he left his booth for a minute to use the restroom. He'd just washed his hands when voices drifting on the breeze through the open window caught his attention. He stilled, hoping no one came into the bathroom to find him standing there, doing nothing but listening.

"…transfer…"

"…not going to like it…police…evidence…"

"…doesn't matter, we can't wait…has to be tonight…"

"…Hurricane Edges."

Then the voices stopped. He hurried back to his table.

"Would you like more coffee, sir?" the ponytailed waitress asked.

"I'd love the check, actually." He was working out in his mind that the voices had come from an alley behind the diner, toward the dock and the main part of downtown. If he hurried maybe he could catch a glimpse of the men he'd overheard, see if he recognized them, or if he could get a picture of anyone to send back to the GBI lab to go through facial recognition software.

"Sure." The waitress nodded, started digging around

in the pockets of her apron. Nate took a deep breath, kept his hands still in his lap rather than drumming on the table with his fingers, like the tension inside him was making him want to do. Seriously, could he just leave a twenty on the table and call it good?

Nate was about to ask that when she finally produced the piece of paper. "Here you go…"

"Thanks." He glanced at it and the total and handed her the receipt along with a twenty. "Thank you—keep the change."

"Have a good night," she called as Nate hurried past.

He pushed the door open into the darkness, then moved around that side of the building without rushing, but making sure he didn't waste any time.

Nothing. There were no people anywhere near the outside of the diner. He'd missed them in the time it had taken to take care of his bill.

He pushed back disappointment. One opportunity missed didn't mean he had to miss the next one, which seemed likely to present itself tonight. Sure, there was a possibility that he conversation he'd overheard was between two ordinary, law-abiding people—but it didn't seem likely, given what they'd said. Far more likely was the idea that they were criminals who would be doing some of their smuggling tonight.

Hurricane Edges. Where was that? And how much time did he have to figure it out? They hadn't mentioned a time. It could be as soon as half an hour from now. Or it could be hours. There was no way of knowing.

When he arrived back at his hotel room, he locked the door behind himself and grabbed the stack of maps of the area he'd bought when he'd started preparing for this assignment. Hurricane Edges…nothing. He couldn't find it anywhere near Treasure Point, not even on the most detailed map of the marsh and tidal creek system that he had.

He thought of the kayaks at the O'Dells' house. Thought of the kayak trips in the marsh near Savannah that he and Claire, Justin and Katie had taken. Claire had always been the most adept at finding the right route. The marsh was something she knew better than the back of her hand.

And if that had been true in Savannah, miles from where she grew up, surely it would be the same in Treasure Point.

If anyone in town knew where Hurricane Edges was, Claire would.

He grabbed the maps, shoved them in a pack and slung it across his chest as he walked out of his hotel room, back to where he'd parked the bike, still running over the plan that was taking shape in his mind.

Nate climbed onto his motorcycle and headed back in the direction of the O'Dells' house, blood pumping through his veins in anticipation of what they might discover. Tonight might be the night they got the break they needed.

He followed the speed limits through town, then pushed them on the back roads, loving the feeling of his bike leaning underneath him as he took the turns. He was going to talk Claire into taking a ride with him one of these days—she might never admit to it, but she'd like it.

When he reached the house, he slowed to a stop, shut the bike down and climbed off.

Nate made his way toward the front door, still working on sorting on the details in his mind. Best case scenario, they'd get close enough to see who was on the boat—maybe giving them names or faces they could identify of who was working on this operation besides the Carson brothers. If there was enough light, he might even be able to get pictures of a few of them, send them in to be run through facial recognition, see if they turned up any hits. The more names the GBI had, the better. Worst case scenario, besides getting caught, would be that they saw nothing. Somewhere in between those two, there were a lot of details they could find out that could build their case.

Nate lifted his hand to the door, but before he could knock, Claire opened it.

"Nate. What's wrong?"

"Can I come in?" She stepped aside, and he walked into the house. "I need you to tell me where Hurricane Edges is."

"Why?"

"I heard some men talking. I think there might be a drug transaction tonight."

"At Hurricane Edges?" Claire looked uncertain. She gazed at Nate and just shook her head. "No way will you be able to find that. Especially not at night."

"Can you just show me? I have to try."

She still seemed to hesitate. Just how hard was this place to find?

"What's wrong, Claire?" Gemma asked from the living room.

"It's Nate. He thinks he has a lead."

"I know I have a lead," he said as he stepped into the living room to explain. "I definitely heard some men talking about an exchange happening tonight, at a specific location. What I don't have is any idea how to get there."

"Where is it?"

"Hurricane Edges."

Gemma winced.

"Even I don't know how to get there." Matt shook his head. "They picked a good spot. It's isolated, hidden. And they don't have to worry about running into anyone because it's dangerous to try to find, all in a tangle of marsh creeks and near enough to open water to be vulnerable to the tide and the waves."

"We wouldn't have to go all the way there, though. Just close. Is there somewhere nearby I could get close enough to get photographs of whoever is involved in this meeting?"

Matt shrugged. "I don't know. I'm sorry."

"Really, you just can't," Gemma insisted. "It's too dangerous. It's only doable if you're very good and very familiar with the area. But for a newcomer like you, and at night? It's foolish."

"It's foolish no matter how well you know the area," Matt muttered. "Even I never tried to get there, and I've done my fair share of ocean kayaking around here."

Nate couldn't just let this lead go. It was the best he had so far, the most promising shot at identifying who else was working with the Carson brothers. And even if the man in charge wasn't on the boat tonight, if he could get clear, unmistakable evidence against the Carson brothers, then it might be the leverage his team needed to get them to make a plea deal.

"They're right," Claire said, breaking into his thoughts. "It's a bad idea. And anyway, there's just no way to explain how to get there. Trust me."

"You already know how to get there."

Claire didn't deny it. All eyes in the room went to her.

"But you don't kayak, do you?" Gemma looked at her, expression a mixture of confusion and hurt at being left out.

"I did in college." Claire looked away and continued talking to Nate. "You'd be lost in the marsh till morning, or worse, end up in open water and be unable to handle your kayak in the waves."

"Hey, what I'm hearing is that you don't trust my kayaking skills." He rarely teased anyone anymore. It just wasn't part of his personality since everything had happened with his sister. But the mood in this room was heavy, and he'd have done almost anything to lighten it.

"Nate. Be serious."

And apparently Claire didn't appreciate the teasing.

He let out a sigh. "Listen, I understand it's hard to get to, Claire, but can you try to map it out for me? I have to go out there."

"I haven't even been since…" She trailed off, like she was thinking of something unpleasant. Then she shook it off. "Since college."

"But you can try to get me there? This could really be the break we need."

She studied him for a minute. Blew out a breath and squared her shoulders. "Let me come with you."

"What?"

"Let me come with you." The same words again, more insistent this time.

"No! I'm not bringing you with me to watch some drug smuggling in action—it's too dangerous."

"So is going out to Hurricane Edges alone, at night, when you don't know the area. It's smarter to have more than one person out there anyway, in case something does go wrong, which is always a good possibility."

"That's why I don't want you to come. I want you safe."

"I want you safe, too." She didn't back down. Nate knew when he'd been beaten.

He nodded slowly. "Okay. You can come, show me where it is. But you're staying back, away from the spot itself."

"I can think of some good places where we can hide."

"You're letting her come?" Gemma shot Nate a look. "You think it's worth putting her in danger?"

"Gemma—" Claire started.

"Gemma, she's already in danger," Matt reminded her. Nate nodded.

"I'm sorry," Nate began. "I understand the risks involved, but right now every moment that these guys aren't caught is a risk for Claire. We don't know the full extent of who is after her, and to be honest, we don't know how to stop them. Every attack against her so far has completely blindsided us. This one risk could carry a lot of reward with it if we could use information we find to figure out who else is involved in this drug ring and build a solid case against them."

"I'm not sure it's my favorite idea…" Matt met Nate's eyes. "But I agree that it's all we've got."

"So she's going?" Gemma still didn't look happy, but Nate didn't blame her. He was still asking himself if he could he really put Claire in a position that carried this much risk.

Then again, she'd been there before and seemed confident that she knew the area well. He trusted her ocean kayaking skills. And as far as the danger from the drug smugglers, the cover they'd been using in town—being a couple—could come in handy if he took Claire with him. Even if they *were* observed, probably no one would see anything other than a man and a woman out enjoying the ocean at night.

Claire would be safe. He thought. He hoped. Because if she wasn't, he didn't know how he'd forgive himself. But he had to try to see this meeting.

"Let's go."

Claire hadn't been out here at night in years, but it was like riding a bike, being on these tidal creeks and rivers. Of course, back when she'd done all that exploring, she'd wanted to memorize everything about Treasure Point so that she'd have strong memories to carry with her when she left it behind for good after college was over. While she'd never admit to her sister or anyone else the degree to which she'd intended to leave for college, visit on breaks, and then never come back after graduation…that had been the plan. Her thirst for adventure, to test her own limits and make something of herself, had been strong. She couldn't have known that it would later battle with the desire for a life without the kind of heartache Justin and his quest—her quest, too—for adventure had caused.

That revelation should also have served as a good reminder for her that Nate Torres was most definitely off-limits. He wasn't a small-town, picket fence guy by any stretch of the imagination. He had a purpose, a mission, which was more than Claire had in life, and she wouldn't ask him to give it up, even if they *were* right for each other. Which they weren't. Being alone with him so often, especially right now, with her heart pounding with adrenaline out in the moonlight, made it easy to feel some sort of attraction. But soon enough, the case would be over. At least, she hoped so, for her safety. Then he'd go back to Atlanta, keep being a big hero at his job, and she'd settle back into the safe life she'd created for herself.

And keep wondering now and then if she was really *living*.

Claire pushed that thought away, reminded herself that even though this place was familiar, it could turn dangerous in a second if one's attention wandered. Tension tightened all her muscles, and Claire was reminded of why she avoided things like this—the uncomfortable way she couldn't take deep breaths, the way her heart pounded.

Of course she was also reminded of why she'd once loved adventures like this. The rush was unbeatable, the excitement like nothing she'd felt lately.

"Go north about ten feet," she whispered to Nate, who sat in the seat behind her.

She slid her paddle into the water on one side and tilted it to the other in a comfortable motion. Nate matched her pace perfectly, and Claire had to smile a little at how natural this seemed. They'd kayaked together years ago, but never in the same kayak. She wouldn't have guessed their strokes would match so perfectly, but now she found herself wondering what it would have been like to share a kayak with Nate back then. What it would have been like if they'd been the ones dating. Would they have had any better chance of making it work than she and Justin had?

No. Everything that had made Justin wrong for her was a quality Nate possessed.

"Where now?"

"Turn right at the clump of marsh grass."

But Claire didn't need to think about Nate tonight anyway, not romantically. Their goals for tonight were to find the rendezvous point Nate had overheard people talking about, get some good intel that Nate could pass on to his colleagues at the GBI and to stay alive.

Claire's senses seemed extrafocused out here. She felt alive down to every pore, aware of everything. Maybe it was because it was so dark she was having trouble seeing, but her other senses were on alert. She could hear the slight breeze blowing through the marsh grass, the delicate sound of their paddles breaking the surface of the water. She heard nothing else, though, which was good. Nate, and Claire, too, hoped that they'd be in place by the time the men came. He hadn't heard a time, so it was impossible to tell when they'd show up.

Claire wanted this to pay off.

The moon had been out earlier, but it had gone behind a cloud. Claire could see it glowing, but it wasn't providing them with much light. On one hand, that would give them a better chance of remaining undetected, but on the other, it made what they were doing that much more foolhardy.

They traveled quietly for a while, the silence broken only by Claire giving Nate directions when he needed them, but that was more and more rare the deeper into the marsh they got. It seemed like he'd learned to feel Claire's motion, judge by the way she was leaning and paddling exactly where she wanted to go, even when the entrance to a new channel or creek arm was small.

They made one more left. "Brace yourself," she warned him, gripping her own paddle tighter. "The turn is coming up, and the path is rougher here." They turned right and instantly the kayak got noticeably difficult to steer as the glassy water turned to a more quickly moving current with some ocean waves and swells.

"We'll want to stop in about twenty feet," she instructed, and he obeyed. The waves tossed the kayak, and Claire had to keep her paddle in the water, alternating sides and adjusting so that they didn't drift from where they wanted to be.

"I don't think we can keep still enough to wait here," she said a minute later. "What if we go inland just a bit? If we go back about fifty yards and then run up on the banks of the marsh, there's enough land there to beach the kayak. Then we can walk out this way and listen."

"Works for me. You know the tides?"

"Like the back of my hand," Claire promised. "And I checked the chart before we left just in case."

"Okay. Let's go."

In sync, they paddled to the spot Claire had suggested, then ran the kayak aground. Claire steadied herself on the boat before climbing out into the soft mud. Nate followed.

"Help me pull the kayak up a little," she said. He did so and then looked to her for direction.

"Let's go just a little farther this way," Claire whispered, reaching out for Nate's hand for purely practical reasons, even if against her better judgment she did like the feeling of his rough hand in hers.

"See? The marsh grass should shelter us this way." She motioned to the direction they planned to watch. "So I think we're safe as far as discovery is concerned."

"We're not very concealed from the back," Nate said, and he was right. The marsh grass did seem to be shorter on the other end of the island, toward where they'd beached and then left the kayak.

"No, but we shouldn't have to worry about that. I don't think anyone's coming up the creek behind us or anything."

"Shh." Nate lifted one finger to his mouth. Claire stilled.

There, approaching from the north, was one of the boats. The other came from the south. They were go-fast boats, just like the ones she'd seen and painted. "That's them," she whispered.

Nate nodded.

Only snatches of conversation floated across the water to them. Claire didn't recognize the voice that was the loudest.

"Can you tell who that is?" she asked Nate in a whisper.

"Sounds like Jesse Carson."

"...meet up..."

"...busy—business meeting downtown..."

It wasn't much, but that last line was enough to work with, and apparently they both knew it because their eyes met when they heard that part.

Nate held a finger in front of his lips again. Mouthed "later." He seemed to be growing more anxious about the possibility of being discovered, but Claire didn't think there was any way that could happen.

Until minutes later when one boat went out to the ocean, out of sight. And the other headed straight in their direction.

The go-fast boat's lights bore down on the river, speeding closer to them by the second. Time slowed down in Claire's head, and she struggled to figure out what to do. She'd heard of people being frozen in fear before, but up until now it had never happened to her. How could her body betray her this way, refusing to move when she needed it to?

Claire looked back at Nate, who was standing maybe three feet away. He had the oddest look on his face, like he was torn, terrified…knew what to do and was somehow struggling to do it, just like she was struggling to move. The difference was that Claire didn't have any idea what to do.

And then, as the roar of the boat's engine grew nearer, Nate closed the distance between them and wrapped his arms around her, lowering his head and bringing hers toward his until their lips met.

And then they kissed, for long, stretched-out seconds, the only kiss Claire could ever remember that made her feel like she was spinning, off balance in the best way imaginable.

Soon the pounding of her heartbeat was louder in her ears than the sound of the boat. It took her a second to realize that that was because it had moved beyond them. Not stopped. The danger had passed, and Nate…

Realization dawned for Claire as Nate pulled away.

"Oh, you were…" She swallowed hard, felt the blush on her cheeks as she thought about how she'd just kissed him back when all he'd been doing was keeping their cover, making the people on the boat assume they were some crazy kids out being romantic. "Yeah, um, good thinking." Claire shook her head, busied herself, rearranged her hair partly behind her ears, since Nate's hands had tousled it worse than the ocean wind had already done.

"We're sitting ducks out here. I didn't want them to

get it in their heads that we were investigating and run us down."

"Run us down." Claire shuddered. She hadn't even considered the possibility that the larger boat might intentionally veer off course and take them out, but Nate was right. If the drug runners had suspected that they were investigating, or noticed that Claire was one of the people on the marsh island, it was doubtful they would still be alive right now.

She took a breath, willed her voice to stay steady even though her insides had turned to some combination of pudding and mush. "Thanks for thinking so fast, then."

Nate nodded. "We need to get back."

But of course they wouldn't discuss the kiss, not really. What was there to say? Nate had only kissed her so they'd stay safe. Never mind that everything about that kiss had said Nate was wrestling with the same kind of emotions she was—ones that certainly weren't smart in their situation, weren't logical at all, but were strong enough to stir up something.

You couldn't fake a kiss that good. Claire was sure of that. But what would come of pursuing it? A relationship between them would be a dead end—they both knew that.

"Yeah." Claire tried her best to put it out of her mind, like Nate apparently had. Two could do that. "We have somewhere to go now, information to follow up on. That's great, isn't it?"

Nate nodded, but his eyes still seemed darker than usual. Troubled. From the kiss? Or something else? She didn't get a chance to ask before he spoke up again. "Is there another way we can go home?"

"Sure. You don't want to go back where the boat went, is that it?"

"Yeah. I wasn't expecting him to come in this direction. Heading back into the woods near Treasure Point, or to a house outside of town, is the last thing I expected that boat to do."

"It surprised me, too."

"So let's take another way back."

"I can do that."

They climbed in the kayak, working together as a team as well as they had on the way there, and Claire guided them back toward the O'Dells' house. Despite how well they clicked in the kayak, the atmosphere between them was tense. Loaded.

A cold spray of salt water hit Claire in the face as their kayak slammed into a wave. She gasped a little.

"You okay?" Nate asked.

She nodded. Cold, but okay. And truthfully, she probably needed that literal splash in the face. That kiss might have stirred up feelings Claire hadn't expected …but that didn't mean it was right. Or that it needed to happen again. Claire needed to let go of any ideas about that. Forever.

ELEVEN

Nate wasn't happy with the way he'd left things with Claire the night before, but he hadn't known what to say. What *was* there to say after a kiss like that?

Unfortunately for both of them, the kiss had said everything. Neither could deny anymore that there was an attraction on both sides. But that didn't mean they should act on it. They were adults. Certainly they could…ignore it.

But Nate was willing to admit that the cold shoulder he'd given her last night had been too much. He'd never meant to be unkind. He'd just needed…space.

This morning, he was ready to apologize, see if he could make things right and they could just move on.

He knocked on the door, ready to pick Claire up so she could walk around the dock with him—another last-ditch effort to find a lead that could help them. It was a plan they'd decided on last night as he'd dropped her off. After a few seconds passed, the door opened, slowly. It was Gemma, and she didn't look happy to see him.

"Want to explain to me why my sister came back here last night looking so upset?"

Nate opened his mouth, but Claire interrupted before he could talk.

"Gemma!" Claire shook her head. "I love you, sis, but I am fine. I told you I was tired last night." Claire shut the door behind her. Shrugged. "Sorry about that. She can be a bit overprotective."

"Ready for a ride on my bike?"

"Not yet." She shook her head, and Nate was relieved. He'd offered as a matter of course, not expecting her to take him up on it. He would have been thoroughly unprepared if she had. After last night's kiss, he wasn't ready to be that close to her again.

"Mind if we take your car, then?"

"Be my guest." She handed him the keys, climbed in without another word and faced the window.

Nate was still rehearsing his apology when his phone rang. "Hello?"

"It's Matt. I found out about that body."

"Yeah?"

A second of silence. "It was Tony Carson."

Nate didn't know how to process that. "Tony."

"Yes."

"Last week. Very near the time Claire says she painted the lights at night."

"So they might be concerned that she witnessed more than a drug run."

"Exactly. They probably think she could have seen them commit murder."

That explained why they were so determined to kill her.

"I've got to go," Matt continued. "We're working a lot of angles over here, trying to figure out if all of this drug stuff ties to Jenni or if her death was just coincidence."

"By all means, keep working, then. Thanks for updating me. Talk to you later."

He turned to Claire. "The dead man was Tony Carson."

"Really?" She blinked back surprise.

"Yep."

"What does this mean for your case?"

"I'm...not sure yet."

"Speaking of the case," Claire began, "we never talked about that conversation we overheard last night. Do you think it means one of them will be at the business meeting tonight?"

"It sounded like that. What *is* the business meeting?"

"The downtown merchants meet semiregularly to discuss different aspects of running a business downtown. Our next meeting is tonight, right before the town boat parade. Want me to go and see if I notice anyone who doesn't belong there, or anything out of the ordinary?"

Nate seemed to consider it. "If we can work out security, yes. It's potentially a solid lead."

"Okay. And the boat parade? I'd like to go to that, too. I haven't missed one, not even when I was in college, so if we can figure out how to make that work without it being dangerous..."

"I'll see what I can do," Nate promised.

The rest of the ride to town didn't take long, but every minute of it plagued Nate. This case had grown more complex with the discovery of the body's identity. Tony Carson... This shattered what Nate had thought he'd known, made the situation they were dealing with about a hundred times more dangerous. He'd suspected that the Carsons weren't running the show, but the idea that they were disposable to the man in charge took things to a whole new level. If the leader was willing to have one of the Carsons taken out, then he was far more powerful than Nate had realized.

And then there was Claire, sitting beside him, her presence reminding him that someone was counting on him. Unlike his sister, whom he couldn't help anymore, Claire needed him. Her life now hung in the balance of this drug war, the one she'd entered purely by accident when she'd seen the lights in the ocean and painted them.

Would he truly be able to protect her when he was so distracted by everything about her, especially the way it had felt to kiss her last night?

Nate wished he could take her back home, put off the apology until later, separate himself from the emotions Claire made him feel. It felt like the only way he could keep it together and do the kind of work he needed to do.

But that wasn't an option. And unfortunately if they were going to walk around the dock together, they were also probably going to have to make it look like he could more than tolerate being around her. Otherwise he looked too much like a bodyguard.

Stuck between two different kinds of dangers—worse than the proverbial rock and hard place—and Nate didn't know which way to go.

I'm going to need some help here, God. You want this to go the way I do, right? Bad guys in jail, Claire safely back in her coffee shop, living her normal life? Me off to find more criminals who need a taste of justice?

No answer came.

He parked the car in front of Claire's shop. There was a good way to keep them both grounded in reality if there ever was one. The shattered window, the memory of the gunshots…all of that would keep their focus where it needed to be. Squarely on this case.

"I hate seeing it like this," Claire muttered.

"I know."

Claire reached to open the car door.

"One more thing." Nate touched her forearm lightly. She looked down at it, then back at him. "Yes?"

"About last night…"

"Don't. Don't say anything, okay? Please? Let's just move on."

He nodded. "Okay." There were so many things he wanted to say. He wanted to apologize, and yet he didn't because he wasn't entirely sorry it had happened.

They started off together for the docks. Nate took a deep breath, tried to remind himself that the gesture wasn't real, that it meant nothing, and then took Claire's hand in his, talking softly as he did. "I can't look like your bodyguard while we're out in town."

She nodded, looking up at him with a smile that would have made anyone watching assume there was something between the two of them. Even though there wasn't…couldn't be.

"So. I looked over the list Matt gave me, and it had all the information about the boats here, but I thought it would help to see them in person, put a picture to what I know from the list."

"Did you bring the list?"

"Would that look natural, to walk around the dock with a list?" Nate laughed.

"True," Claire admitted. "Do you want me to just tell you who owns which boats as we pass them? Or how do you want to do this?"

That made sense to him. "Yes. And be sure to let

me know any of them that you aren't sure about, especially if you think they might be new here. We'll look them up later."

"How will we remember them? We can't exactly take pictures of them."

He cracked a small smile. "Obviously. But I doubt there will be that many. We'll remember."

She shook her head. "If you say so."

They stepped onto the rough wood of the dock, and Nate glanced without meaning to at the place where Tony Carson's body had washed onto the shore.

Tony Carson, dead. The thought was going to mess with his mind for a while.

"This one," Claire said, tugging him forward, "I've always loved."

Nate whistled. The very first boat was a beauty all right. *The Dixie Queen.* "I can see why. Who owns this one?" It was a model made for speed and luxury and wasn't unlike the profile they were looking for.

Claire laughed. "It's my parents' boat."

Nate laughed too and shook his head. "What about this one?" He motioned to the next one.

"That one belongs to Jerry Hollings—he owns the grocery store in town."

They kept walking. She told him that the sailboat on the left was the property of one of the elders at the church in Treasure Point. The other speedboat he looked at suspiciously belonged to her eighth-grade math teacher's husband.

So far every boat had been accounted for as owned by someone Claire couldn't picture being a killer. At this point, though, Nate was pretty sure they had to discount the idea that the killer was someone they'd be able to identify easily. If he or she was *anyone* with a business downtown, it was going to be someone that would be a surprise to Claire.

So he tried to pay attention to all of the boats, and thought about the ones they'd seen last night—especially the one that had tried to run them down. He'd been too busy making sure their cover stayed intact to look at that boat's name as it passed—something he regretted, but not too deeply. They'd both come out of that situation alive. That was the most important thing.

Although solving this case was going to help that stay possible, so really both were important.

Nate had given up on this excursion yielding anything new, and was beginning to hope that the meeting that night would shed more light on the possibilities, because it wasn't looking like anything was going to catch Claire's eye here, or his.

"Wait." Claire stopped directly in front of an empty slip.

"What?"

"This slip. I'm pretty sure all the slips were full one of the nights that I was on my deck painting—one of the nights the lights didn't show up."

"I don't remember seeing the boat dock in the picture with the 'ocean lights.'" He made quotes with his fingers.

"No, it was another painting."

"And why would it be odd for this slip to have a boat in it?"

"This slip belonged to a guy named Harry. He was arrested a few years ago. Since then, no one else has rented the slip. So until someone else needs it…it's just been open."

"But not one of the nights a couple of weeks ago."

"Exactly." Claire's expression was serious.

"So where's that painting?"

"I have it in my apartment, underneath my painting table. I couldn't quite get the moonlight the right color, so I haven't displayed it yet. It's not one of the ones we looked at the other night. It's in a stack with pieces I was still working on."

Chills shuddered up Nate's spine. "And that's possible evidence."

Claire tugged her hand out of Nate's and hurried down the dock back toward the apartment.

"Claire, wait!" Nate yelled.

The look she threw him was pure irritation.

"You can't just rush in there," he reminded her softly, but in a voice that he hoped she would take seriously.

"Why? You'll be right behind me."

"Too many factors have changed. Everything is even more dangerous than it was two days ago, if you can believe that. It's unstable."

"Okay, so we'll go together."

Nate was already shaking his head. "I need to go in alone."

"Yeah, because that will look so natural."

She had him there, and Nate hated that she was right. He took a deep breath, exhaled and held out his hand again. "Stay close."

She came as close against his side as she could. Nate couldn't say she didn't take direction well.

Claire unlocked the coffee shop when they reached the door. Nate went in first but didn't let go of Claire's hand, so they were both inside quickly.

"Everything is the same as we left it," she whispered. "See?"

"If you don't believe me that there could be a threat here, then why are you whispering?"

Another glare. "I don't know."

They made their way to the stairs in the back and followed them up.

As soon as Nate opened to the door to the apartment, he knew he'd been right to be worried.

Claire's apartment was trashed. Ransacked, vandalized...he couldn't tell which yet, and it would take a careful assessment to decide what, if anything, had been taken. But someone who wasn't Claire and wasn't law enforcement had been here. Carefully he walked farther inside, letting go of Claire's hand so he'd be ready if it became necessary to draw his weapon. "Stay right with me," he told her.

They walked through the kitchen, into the living room and then stopped. The damage was worst in here.

Claire's eyes widened and she pointed to the corner, which was oddly empty compared to the rest of the room, which had debris all over.

"My entire painting desk, supplies...paintings in progress. All of it's gone."

"Someone's been in here since the night you were poisoned."

She nodded. "I wonder if they realized later there might be more in here that could be used as evidence? Or if he'd meant to do all of this that first night, but ran out of time when I woke up?"

"There's no telling." Chills snaked down Nate's spine. "But Claire, we're getting out of here now." His eyes scanned the room. It felt like there was an active threat somewhere, but he didn't know...

"Wait, they left one painting! Right here on the couch. Odd, right? I don't know if they decided this one didn't matter, or—" Claire reached for it, moved it slightly.

"Stop!"

She froze. The painting was still on the couch, but at the very edge, Nate could see something underneath it. Something that looked like the edge of a detonator switch.

"It's a bomb. Claire, come with me now. Slowly."

"Slowly?"

"We're on the top floor. We can't afford to shake anything. Look at the painting. See that black underneath the edge where you moved it?"

Her eyes widened. Face paled. "Yes."

"If it's what I think it is, that's a detonator switch, the kind that explodes once the pressure on it is released. The painting is pushing the switch down, and if you'd picked it up..."

She was backing up slowly now.

"Good job. Keep it steady."

The painting moved a fraction of a centimeter. From its angle, Nate felt a sinking certainty that it was going to continue to shift until it tipped over. Apparently the little bit Claire had moved it was too much.

"Okay." He kept his voice steady. *Don't let her panic, God.* "It's moving too much. We're going to run outside, take cover as far away as we can. Got it?"

"Now?" Claire's voice was shaking, but she kept moving slowly away, just as he'd told her to.

"Now."

She spun on her heel and reached for his hand. He took hers as they both ran for the back door.

The blast hit when they were across the deck, almost to the fire escape stairs. Concussive noise hit, pushing the air in a violent burst of explosive anger.

"Down!" Nate yelled, pulling her with him.

The only place to go was the staircase, and as they went down, they tumbled half a flight of stairs before coming to rest on the landing. The building continued to shake even seconds after the blast, and the deafening thunder of the initial explosion was replaced with the crackle of flames.

Nate knew without looking that the apartment was totally destroyed.

He glanced over at Claire, her face inches from his. His arm was across her back. "Are you okay?"

She nodded. "I think so."

She seemed as surprised by it as he was.

He nodded. "Good." He pulled his eyes away from her deep brown ones, because staring into them right now was making him feel things for her that he wasn't sure he was ready to feel. For one thing, they lived in different worlds. He had his job, she had her coffee shop...

Nate winced. Maybe not after that explosion.

But she did have her town. A family. A life here. She'd made it clear that this was the life she wanted. And if she could have a life like this, one in which she could find peace, Nate didn't want to pull her away from it. He'd take that option for his own life if he could. But Melanie's death had made sure that would never be an option for him. There would always be another dealer, another drug smuggling ring to be dealt with. And as long as he was good at his job, he would keep doing it. Evil couldn't win. He couldn't let it.

Nate slid his arm off her back, rolled away from her and stood up slowly, making sure he hadn't been seriously injured in the fall.

Claire did the same.

Nate pulled out his phone. Dialed 911. "Claire Phillips's apartment just exploded."

"Yes, we've gotten calls from her neighbors. Officers are en route."

He slid the phone into his pocket. Then he glanced over to check on Claire. She looked…

Her hair was messy, light brown with golden highlights like she was made for the beach. Her white fitted sweater was dusty and there was a hole in her jeans, with what looked like blood staining the knee.

"You're not okay. You're hurt."

"It's a scratch. I'll get it checked out if it's bothering you."

She gave him a funny expression, like she was asking him something with her eyes. He didn't have any answers for her. Yes, he was probably disproportionately concerned about a scraped knee.

But it was Claire, and the thought of her getting hurt at all…

He wouldn't have guessed it would affect him so deeply. This wasn't just a case for him. Claire was anything but a case.

She was an old friend. Had been his friend's girlfriend. Someone who loved her town, loved leading a quiet life. But loved rock climbing, kayaking. She was more of a mystery than he could ever hope to solve in a lifetime.

Lifetime?

He didn't know where that thought had come from. It wasn't one he had the luxury of considering, not in a line of work with such a limited life expectancy. He wouldn't do that to a woman, wouldn't do that to Claire especially. It was why he never dated.

Nate heard the sirens as the police approached, then the slamming of doors and pounding of feet as they ran up the stairs.

"Fire department is on their way," Clay Hitchcock said as he came up the stairs. "I'm sorry, Claire, but it looks like a loss from the front. We're here to secure the scene. And after the flames are out and the fire chief says we can go in, we'll send in a crime scene team, see if we can recover any evidence. That's about all we can do."

"I understand."

The explosion added yet another complication in a case that had become nothing but tangles of evil and crime he couldn't quite seem to sort out. But he *had* to, and faster. Because if things kept escalating at the rate they were now, Claire could be running out of time.

TWELVE

By this point, having the police come to her apartment to process a scene was feeling familiar to Claire—so much so that when they said she didn't need to stay and answer any questions, Claire asked Nate if he wanted to leave with her. She knew when the police were done with the scene, she'd need to deal with insurance, process the fact that nearly everything she owned had been destroyed, but for now she just wanted to get away from the place, figure out who was behind this and stop him.

Nate didn't seem to mind leaving either, so they got into her car—thankfully undamaged by the explosion—and headed back to Gemma and Matt's house—the only place Claire really wanted to go.

"Why is this person so fixated on me?" Claire asked Nate after they'd been sitting in the living room drinking coffee for a few minutes.

He shook his head. "You've seen a lot more than you think you have, it looks like. This is now two paintings of yours that could potentially be used in a case against these people. Not to mention, they think you might have witnessed them committing murder."

"I don't want to think about it right now. Let's talk about something else."

"Like what?"

"I don't know." She forced out a laugh, hoping it would lighten the mood. "What was your childhood like? Those kinds of things. You never really talked about your family much when we were in college."

"I don't really like to talk about the past."

Was it her imagination or had Nate actually scooted slightly away from her? Claire let it go, along with her questions about his past. "All right, not that, then. How about the future? What do you want to do with your life? This job forever?"

"Good questions." Nate seemed to consider it as he topped off his own coffee mug from the insulated carafe. "I don't see myself being a GBI agent forever. Eventually you get too old for this kind of field work and start making mistakes that cost people their lives." Claire thought she saw a weird expression on his face—one she'd noticed before when he'd talked about his job, but she wasn't sure enough to say anything. Besides, she'd probably pried enough for one night. "So I think eventually I see myself working on narcotics still, but in a crime lab or a supervisor capacity."

"Do you have to go back to school for that? You majored in criminal justice, right?"

Nate shook his head. "Double major—criminal justice and chemistry, so I'd be fine. I got my master's in criminology after that."

That was an impressive amount of education. She'd known he was a good student, but they'd been in completely different fields, so they'd never had any classes together. She hadn't realized just how well-educated he really was. Especially compared to her, who had barely managed to pass her classes junior year, after the accident.

She was quiet then, suddenly self-conscious. Not that she felt like an education defined a person. But Nate was so impressive in more ways than one that she suddenly felt silly sitting here, trying to have a normal conversation with him, like they were still friends or something, when to him she was a case. The girl next door, nothing more.

"That's all you want to know?"

Claire looked up at him, found that the teasing expression on his face matched the tone of his voice. "No, you can keep going."

"Well, for someone who kept asking questions a minute ago, you sure quit awfully fast. Are you okay?"

She nodded. "I'm fine. So the lab, huh?"

"I want to stay involved, keep working to take down as many people responsible for ruining innocent lives with drugs as I can."

"Because of..." Claire trailed off. Bringing his sister up was probably a bad idea.

"Because of my sister, yeah."

"What exactly..." She found her curiosity had made a sudden comeback. "What happened to her? You said it was drugs, but..."

Nate glanced at his watch. "Only two hours until the business meeting. Are you ready for it?"

Apparently they were done talking.

"I'm mostly ready."

"And don't forget the boat parade tonight."

How could Claire forget? It had always been one of her favorite traditions at this time of year—something about the glowing lights reflecting off the water had always been so beautiful to her. In fact, that was probably what had gotten her into trouble in the first place. The lights on the ocean at night that had started this whole thing were so similar—that was why she'd wanted to paint them as soon as she'd seen them.

And why the boat parade held very little appeal at the moment. "You know…" she began, "I'm not sure I want to go. Maybe I'll stay here this year."

"I have a hard time believing that the boat parade isn't your kind of thing." Nate raised one eyebrow in amusement, but Claire couldn't handle the teasing expression right now. The day had been too much, it felt too hopeless that this nightmare would ever be over, and she just needed…she wasn't sure what.

"Well, here I am, surprising people again." She wasn't proud of her sarcastic tone, but her emotions were raw, and her mind felt swirled around, unable to focus on anything.

Except the one horrible truth it kept landing on— someone wanted her dead.

Claire stood up from the couch, brushed her hands on her pants and paced toward the window, then back again. "Look, that's not true, okay? I usually love the boat parade. But everything's different now."

Nate nodded, his face having grown more serious when Claire started overreacting. Already she felt bad for snapping at him. "Listen," she said, "I'm sorry for how I said it."

"It's understandable. Claire, I know I'm asking a lot of you in this case. It's not necessarily standard protocol to allow a citizen so much involvement in an undercover investigation, but it has worked out perfectly for both of us, as perfectly as a situation like this could have. We'll find the criminals much faster this way, I'm sure of it. But I know it's taking a toll on you. And I appreciate that you're brave and strong enough to do it anyway."

It was costing her; it was true.

"I think I need a quick break before the meeting tonight," she said.

"What were you thinking of?"

"A nap, maybe."

"You go, take a quick nap, and then you can head to the meeting. I think I've worked out what to do about that, by the way."

"Oh?"

Nate nodded. "I'm going to ask the Treasure Point Police Department to station a couple of officers there, against the back wall. I'll be watching you until you go inside, and then they'll be protecting you. Since this level of criminal activity isn't the norm for Treasure Point, I don't think anyone will bat an eye at the police department wanting a higher-level of presence than normal."

"Perfect. That sounds good." Her safety seemed so important to him, and unless Claire was mistaken, it wasn't really part of his job description. Either he was doing it as a favor for the Treasure Point PD, or he was doing it for her.

Whichever it was, it made her heart smile, even if her face felt too tired and scared to do the same. Despite the tough exterior and the slight tendency toward brooding, Nate Torres was a good guy. She'd known that all along, of course, but in the wake of everything that had happened with Justin, it had been easier to walk away from his friendship that came with so many bittersweet memories. She was glad they'd had a chance to reconnect, now that enough time had gone by for her to be able to leave the past in the past.

"See you soon." Claire headed up the stairs, lay down on the guest bed she'd claimed for the time being and closed her eyes.

When the alarm she'd set for four thirty woke her up, she felt as if she could see more clearly, like her mind was less foggy than it had been earlier. She was ready for the meeting.

"How are you feeling?" Nate asked as soon as she came down the stairs.

"I'm ready for this," Claire assured him. "If I let it, it would mess with my mind that I'm probably going to be in the room with someone who wants me dead, but thinking about that right now isn't going to do me any good, you know?"

"You're right. Don't think about it. You'll be completely safe there between the public location and the officers in the back."

Claire still couldn't shake her uneasiness entirely—but she trusted Nate.

She really did. Yes, he was like Justin in a lot of ways. The same thrill-chasing personality, the same willingness to put himself at risk. But there was a steadiness to Nate that Justin had never had. He might take chances with his own life, but she was sure he'd never take chances with hers.

"Let's drive my car," Claire said before he could offer to take his bike. "I need a little extra in the safe feelings department."

"You've got it," Nate said.

They walked outside, climbed into the car and drove toward town.

The large building where the downtown business owners' meetings were held was half-full by the time Claire walked inside. Alone. She took a deep breath but let it out when she noticed the officers in the back. She took a seat as close to them as she could and looked around.

There was Lucas, who owned the Italian restaurant at the corner of downtown farthest from the dock. Marcy, who ran the diner. Greg from the bookstore. Brad from the bike rental shop. Betsy from the most adorable clothing boutique in the South. Steven from the car repair shop. Pearl from the stationery store. Andrew from the drugstore. Jerry from the grocery store. Those were the ones who had shops closest to Claire's or stores she frequented most often, but there were ten or so others whom Claire had seen in passing but just didn't know as well.

Greg, who was usually in charge at meetings like this, went to the front and called the meeting to order. Claire did the best she could to pay attention, but scenes from the case that had brought them to this point kept flashing in her mind. The lights at night. Hands grabbing her off the street. Gunshots fired at her. Voices on the boat when she and Nate were in the marsh. This room, right here, fully lit up and with a friendly enough atmosphere, but dangerous in reality if she could only look into the hearts of everyone in this room.

Claire barely heard a word that was said. She'd have to ask Greg to email her a copy of the meeting minutes later.

Greg. Could it be him? It could. Just as easily as it could have been anyone else.

There was no way for Claire to be sure. She'd tell Nate she'd done her best, but much as she scanned their faces, tried to think of past interactions with them, or any weird tics that might give away their guilt now, Claire saw…nothing. Just fellow townspeople whom she considered to be friends.

The meeting passed quickly. Claire stood to leave as soon as it was finished and Steven, the car repair guy, asked her a question about the boat parade. She barely stuttered out an answer. She reacted the same when Betsy from the clothes boutique—who'd been sitting just a few chairs down—complimented her shoes. And when Brad from the bike shop smiled and waved.

She was seeing suspects everywhere and nowhere all at the same time.

Like it or not, Claire felt she and Nate had to go to the boat parade. Even if she wasn't sure she felt like enjoying the event, it could turn up a clue. And it would undoubtedly give them another chance to watch some of the people they'd been suspecting, since almost everyone in this room was planning to get dinner and then go to the parade.

Claire hurried down the stairs and straight to her car, where Nate was waiting. "Thanks for being here," she said to him as soon as she climbed in.

"Of course. I wouldn't have left you."

She believed he meant it, and it felt like warm coffee inside her heart. Or maybe like fresh cinnamon rolls.

Not something she could think about right now, not when so much was riding on this moment. She needed to stay focused on the case. Since the meeting had yielded nothing interesting, they couldn't waste any time.

"I didn't learn anything," she told him as they drove back toward the O'Dells' house for dinner. They still had several hours until the parade started, and Gemma had promised to make low-country boil—shrimp, sausage, potatoes and corn. It didn't get any better or more Treasure Point than that. "I spent the entire meeting on hyperalert trying to figure out who could be behind it, trying to make sure I didn't miss anything. But everyone seemed normal."

"Not surprising. Whoever's behind this has a lot of experience at keeping up a facade. It was a long shot, but since we heard that he or she was going to be there, we couldn't just ignore it." Nate reached over and squeezed the hand that Claire was resting on the shifter. "We'll figure it out."

She looked down at their hands, both tanned, but his rough like he'd done plenty of work with his hands in his lifetime, and hers smaller, more delicate, even though she kept her nails short like someone who worked with dough all the time. The hands of a GBI agent from the city and a coffee shop owner and consummate small-town girl. It didn't get much more opposite than that.

Claire cleared her throat. "I can give you a list of most of the people who were there, though. No one was missing that I noticed. I did make a mental note of that."

Nate nodded, slipped his hand off hers. "So did you change your mind about the boat parade tonight?"

"I did. I think we should go, just in case."

"There could be a lead there."

"Right, and we can't risk missing something we should investigate further just because I don't feel as much like enjoying the parade as I usually do."

"Besides…" Nate's voice had a smile it in, so Claire glanced over. His face was smiling, too. "The lights will be pretty, and there's no one I'd rather look at them with than you."

* * *

After dinner, they were almost back to town when traffic thickened. "Is the boat parade always this popular?" Nate asked. "I hadn't expected this many cars." It was a lame topic of conversation, but anything that would return them to the easy repartee they'd had earlier would work for him right about now.

"It's one of the town's most popular events. People travel here from Savannah, Darien and Brunswick."

Nate heard the town pride in her voice, and it made him smile even as it reminded him one more time that Claire was Treasure Point through and through. When this case was over, which he hoped would be soon for her safety, there was a good chance they would never see each other again.

Never had he been so torn about wrapping up a case.

"I'm looking forward to seeing it, then" was all he said. Claire navigated the car through traffic without saying anything else, either, and they parallel parked in a spot away from the coffee shop, near a bookstore.

"You didn't want to park near your place?"

"For one thing, those spots are even closer to the dock, so they're pretty popular. I doubt there would be any left now. For another, no, I don't want to be near my building."

"Why?"

She shook her head. "Whoever's after me seems to have been there more than I have lately."

"You're going to have to go back eventually. You remember that, right?"

"Theoretically." She gave him a small smile that had a hint of teasing to it, like Claire really did know that one day she would have to bounce back, move on.

But first they had to eliminate the threat to her life.

"Thanks for bringing me to this tonight," Nate said as he reached for the door handle, before opening the door. "I could have come by myself but it wouldn't have been nearly as fun."

"I hope I can help you uncover something."

Her focus was better than his at this point, apparently. But Nate nodded, because even though he was also looking forward to spending the evening with Claire, he hoped it helped in their investigation, too.

"Do you have a preference for where we watch?" Claire asked him.

"Somewhere we have a good view. Not isolated but not overrun with crowds, either, if that's possible."

She was already nodding. "I'll just take you where I usually go." Claire held his hand and led him just past the docks, up a small hill to a playground overlooking the harbor. There were a few kids with their parents nearby, but for the most part it was quieter here than down by the docks.

"Perfect," he said as they settled on a bench.

"It's the best view. Well, besides being in the parade," Claire added with a laugh. "Oooh, look, it's starting!"

The first boat was an impressive shrimp boat, obvious from its large beams that stretched out on either side. The owners had decorated almost every square inch of the boat in lights and spelled out A Treasure Point Christmas in contrasting colors on the side.

"The Bryans usually start the parade," Claire said softly.

The next boat was smaller but no less well decorated. This one was a houseboat, or something with a cabin, anyway, and had inflatable reindeer and Santa taking off from its roof.

"People really go all out here, don't they?" Nate commented. "And what did you mean about being in it? Just a comment, or have you really been before?"

Claire nodded. "Gemma and I used to ride with our parents when they did it." She pointed. "See that one, about three boats back, off in the distance? That's their boat. Matt and Gemma are driving it tonight since my parents are still out of town."

Nate followed her gaze, then squinted a little.

"That boat a few down from theirs in the parade. Whose is that?"

"Brad Reid. He owns the bike rental shop. Why?"

"So he was at that meeting earlier. The one we heard the men talking about last night. Where you just went to see if you could find anyone who seemed suspicious."

"Brad? No. That's crazy. Besides, why would you say it was him?"

"His boat. Was it one of the ones we saw in the boat slips earlier today?"

Claire shook her head. "No. He has a house on the water, so he doesn't dock it in town."

"Then why can't it be his boat that ran us down? Look at it, Claire."

He pointed, and she followed his gaze. Nate looked at the boat for another minute to make sure he wasn't seeing things, but no, even from this far away he could see the dent in the lower part of the boat, the same one he'd noticed last night in the marsh. The only difference was that this boat had numbers above that dent. Nate was pretty sure, though, that if he could see the boat in the daylight, there would be some evidence of adhesive where something had been taped over those numbers the night before to make the boat less identifiable.

But Nate was used to having to look beyond the obvious.

"Do you see that dent?" He looked over at her, saw that she'd noticed the boat he was referring to. "The large one near where the water comes up to?"

"Yeah."

"I saw that on the boat last night."

"I didn't see anything."

"This is what I do, Claire—notice details. And I'm telling you, it adds up. Come on, let's go. Back to your car."

"What? Where are we going?"

"I want to see that boat closer up. Where else can we go to see the parade that would give us a closer vantage point?"

Claire hurried after him. "Lookout Bluff, maybe? It's north of town." When they reached the car, she climbed into the driver's seat without offering Nate the keys. "It's easier if I get us there. What are you hoping to see, if you're so sure it's his boat?"

"I'm not sure yet," Nate admitted. "But if I can get a picture of his boat, that could come in handy. The people back at the GBI lab are pretty impressive with technology. There's a chance we could tie this boat to other suspicious transactions, or at least track where it's been somehow."

"We still have to figure out why they killed that other guy—Tony Carson. You don't think that was Brad, do you?"

"Yes and no," Nate said. "I'm not sure it was him, personally, but it might have been on his orders. If we can prove he's involved in anything illegal at all, we can get him in jail and then work on figuring out what all he's been involved in beyond that."

"That makes sense."

She pulled the car into a little gravel parking lot. Nate noticed that they weren't the only ones there.

"So is this…"

Claire was already opening the door. "Let's go. I don't want to lose them, either. And yes, it's kind of a make out spot."

Nate couldn't help but laugh at the irony in that. They'd spent all day together, pretending to be a romantic couple, and now they were at the town's romantic rendezvous spot, but they were using it to catch a glimpse at a boat that was being used in the drug trade.

They reached the edge of the bluff just as the boat was coming by. Yes, it was definitely the same one that had almost run them down in the marsh. Speedboat style, which was common enough, but that dent on the starboard bow left no doubt in Nate's mind. He snapped a few pictures with the camera he'd brought for the boat parade—which allowed him to zoom in. Not even sure what he was capturing, he just kept snapping frames until the boat was out of sight. He hadn't seen Brad, but Nate wouldn't think it would be hard to get a picture of him to the GBI lab, either.

He'd send these pictures tonight as soon as he got back to his hotel room.

They stared in silence as the boat turned back toward town, too far out for Nate to notice anything else.

"I'm guessing you need to get back," Claire said.

Nate nodded. "I think it's time to put in a call to my boss again and see how he wants me to handle this new development. I also need to talk to the Treasure Point PD, get into the computer database and see if the boat is registered to Brad."

"Why wouldn't it be?"

"You just never know where the next lead will come from." Nate shook his head. "We have to follow up on everything. I also need to look deeper into Brad, figure out where he fits if I can." Nate exhaled, feeling…he didn't know what. The parade, the sparkling lights on the water and then the sudden adrenaline rush of chasing the boat…the night had taken so many more twists and turns than he could have anticipated, and he didn't know how to handle them.

Claire didn't seem to, either. She wasn't the reserved Claire she'd been when he showed up in her town, not quite, but neither was she the adventurous version of herself he'd been friends with years ago.

Nate wanted to get to know her better, wanted to know which was the real Claire. Help her be that.

Unfortunately, whichever way this case went—if it picked up the pace and he figured out who was behind everything *or* if it dragged out—he wasn't the right guy for her, never had been, never would. Even if some part of him almost wanted to be.

THIRTEEN

Everything about the boat parade had made Claire want to paint it. In fact, she wasn't sure why she hadn't tried before. The lights on the boats, the darkness of the sky, and the gentle blending of all the colors of Christmas lights on the water made for a scene that would translate well to canvas if only she could capture it.

But thinking of painting only reminded her of the currently empty corner of her destroyed apartment, about why it was empty. So instead, she'd shoved the thoughts aside, into a corner of her mind reserved for things she shouldn't think about. Painting. Someone wanting her dead. The fact that she couldn't quit wondering if Nate Torres might ever see her as something other than a damsel in distress.

The unfortunate thing was that in her effort to police what she thought about, Claire was afraid she'd come off a little awkward all night. Too much on her mind… too little…whichever it was, she hadn't felt like herself.

So when Nate had to take her home early and pursue the lead with the boat's owner's name and registration, she hadn't protested.

He was working in Matt's office right now, since

Matt and Gemma were still at the parade and Claire wasn't eager to be alone in the woods. When she hadn't feared for her life, she'd found the surroundings out here peaceful—the edge of woods with Southern live oaks that overhung the house in places, and the marsh leading to a tidal creek just fifty yards or so from the front door.

Right now? Claire didn't want to think about how ideal this location was for someone to attack her. *If* she was alone. Which she wasn't, because Nate was looking out for her.

Claire had told him good-night earlier and headed up to the guest room. She'd tried to read for a little while, but she'd been unable to focus on that, either. "Father God, what's wrong with me? Why can't I focus?" Claire whispered the prayer softly but felt it with all her heart. No answer came immediately, but that was okay. She'd keep listening.

For now, she'd go to sleep. Try not to think about...

Whatever it was she was avoiding thinking about.

When Claire opened her eyes next, it was fully light inside the room. In December, light didn't come terribly early, so she must have slept later than she'd meant to. Claire glanced at the clock. Past eight—way behind schedule for her. Nate would probably arrive soon. She showered and dressed in record time, letting her wet hair hang down her back.

"Sorry I'm up so late," she said to Gemma when she'd gotten downstairs. Claire stifled a yawn and reached for the coffee mug her sister was handing to her.

"You don't have to be sorry. You were probably exhausted."

It was true. She had been. Already she was feeling better this morning.

Claire would have to see if that held up after she saw Nate. These last few days, just being around him seemed to short-circuit something in her mind. Much as she wanted to tell herself to use her common sense and acknowledge they weren't a good fit for each other, she had a feeling her heart wouldn't listen.

Besides, the last time she'd given someone a "he's all wrong for you" speech, it had been her sister. And look how well Gemma and Matt had turned out.

Not that everyone was guaranteed that kind of fairy-tale ending.

"When's Nate coming back? Do you know?" Claire tried to ask it casually, but the smirk Gemma gave her said she hadn't been entirely successful.

"He's in the guest house. We got home so late last night we told him he should just stay for the night and go back to the hotel today."

Matt'd had a guest house built after he and Gemma got engaged so that they would have more options for company once they decided to start a family. It was set far enough back from the house to give guests privacy.

"He's here?" Claire glanced at the coffee Gemma had poured and slid over to her in her favorite seashell mug, and then looked back at the stairs. Maybe she should go dry her hair.

She heard a knock on the front door at exactly that moment. Either she had to make a run for it now and let her coffee get cold, or Nate would see her looking… well, imperfect.

"Don't you dare move." Gemma's voice didn't leave much room to argue, so Claire took another sip of coffee and tried to stop her leg from bouncing up and down as her sister went to let Nate inside.

"Good morning," she heard her sister say.

"Morning. I thought I'd see if there was coffee. Hope you don't mind."

Claire didn't want to notice that his voice was deeper in the morning, rougher around the edges. But it was.

"Not at all." Gemma hurried back into the kitchen and poured him a cup.

Claire kept her eyes fixed on the coffee in her cup.

"Morning, Claire."

Well, if he was going to talk to her directly, then she couldn't ignore him no matter how tangled up he made her feel inside. She looked up at him, noticed the shadow of a beard around his jawline. He was smiling, just a little, and it felt directed at her. "Good morning," she managed to say without stumbling over the words.

Weeks. The man had been in town for weeks and she'd been fine. She'd even handled that kiss—Claire took a big sip of coffee in an attempt to not think about it in detail—fairly well. But one boat parade with him, and somehow she'd managed to start…what?

Falling for him? No…she couldn't be. Right?

All she knew was that lately, she'd started looking at him like she'd never looked at him before, like she'd never looked at any man before. Not even Justin.

God? What's going on here?

"You okay?" he asked, oblivious to her turmoil.

"I'm fine." Another smile, another sip of coffee. See, if she just focused, she'd be fine. "What's the plan for today?"

Nate slid one of the barstools out and sat down. "We're going to move in closer. I talked to the chief early this morning, and he is calling a meeting in about an hour to assign a special group of officers to surveillance duty."

"You think Brad is really the key to this?"

"Maybe, maybe not. But the more people we know who are connected to the smuggling ring, the greater the chances are that we can get all of them. And be positive we've got the guy who's over it all calling the shots."

"Makes sense."

"I'm leaving now, with Matt. There's an officer right outside on the front porch who is assigned to you for the day. The chief insisted, with the way everything keeps escalating."

"Okay, I'll see you soon. Go get them."

The early morning buzz at the police department reminded Nate of being back at GBI headquarters. Everyone had goals for the day, angles to follow up on, but most of them grabbed coffee first, told each other their plans. It was a familiar routine that had been true in every law enforcement office Nate spent any time in during his career.

"Everyone here?" the chief asked gruffly. The table in the break room held the chief, Nate, O'Dell, Hitchcock, and Officer Logan, a guy Nate had seen in passing but didn't know well.

"Lieutenant Davies is going to handle whatever comes in today that isn't related to this case or to Jenni's murder. It appears that Agent Torres was correct, and the two of those are linked."

Agent Torres. Wow, he'd been undercover for so long that it was odd to hear that title used. Wade usually just called him Torres. Better for him not to get in the habit of calling him *agent* lest that come back to bite Nate in a deep cover investigation.

The chief continued.

"Fingerprints on a piece of evidence—a pouch of tools—that was dropped at Claire Phillips's apartment are a match to Brad Reid. He wasn't in our local AFIS system, but when Shiloh ran the prints, he came up in the FBI database. O'Dell, you patrol Treasure Point, specifically looking for anything suspicious related to this case. Don't respond to anything less serious than assault. The other officers under Davies's command today can handle that. You just see if Brad does any business with anyone else in town. Got it?"

The chief moved his gaze to the next man at the table.

"We'll put Hitchcock near Brad's shop in a patrol car, ready to follow him if he leaves from there. Someone else on the beach on a bike…" The chief looked over at Officer Logan.

"Put the new guy on bike duty," Logan said. "Sure." His words were sarcastic, but the grin on his face betrayed how excited he was. If Nate had to guess, he'd say the guy was twenty-one at most, likely on his first big case. That kind of enthusiasm could be helpful, or it could be dangerous. They'd see how it shook out at the end of this case.

"Agent Torres." The chief looked at Nate. "You stay with Claire."

"Sir…"

"I can't have you driving a department vehicle. It's an insurance liability, not to mention it would destroy your cover. And you're not going to chase a suspect down on a motorcycle, not in my jurisdiction. This is important, and we need to wrap it up as soon as possible, but I haven't lost an officer in the line of duty in all the years I've been working here and I'm not going to start now, especially not with someone else's officer. Am I clear?"

Here they were, maybe at the final chase…and they wanted to take Nate out of it? Hadn't this been his case to start with?

Nate had nothing against the Treasure Point Police Department. Especially for a small department, they did a thorough job and he trusted their skills.

But this was a personal war. No, Brad Reid hadn't been the one to make the drug that killed his sister. But the story felt familiar. He didn't want anyone else's sister to be killed because of this drug.

He wanted to be the one to end this.

"All right, head to where I've stationed you."

Everyone stood and moved toward the door.

"Agent Torres," the chief called to him. Nate walked over, shoved his hands in his pockets and reminded himself to keep his mouth shut for now.

"We're more equipped for a chase than you are. That's all this is about. You are still handling this case, and we know you know much more about the Carsons' operation than we do. We need you on this, need your cooperation. You understand?"

"Yes, sir." And he did. Everything the chief said was right. It didn't mean Nate had to be happy about it.

"So today you focus on keeping Claire safe—and distracted from all the horrible things that have happened to her, if you can."

"I'll do my best."

"Maybe even get her out of town."

Nate looked over at the chief. "If you think it's going

down today, I don't want to be out of town and unable to get back in time."

"This is more than a case to you, isn't it?"

He didn't deny it.

"Because of Claire?"

He started to shake his head. Ever since he'd been assigned to investigate the Carson brothers, Nate had been thinking of his sister. But at this point... He hesitated. Shrugged. "I don't know, sir. Although the idea of someone messing up her life like this..."

"Doesn't sit well, does it? Claire's never done anything to hurt anyone. Just runs that shop and minds her own business. The town loves her. I'm sure you can see that."

They did love her, Nate knew. But he wanted to say that they loved only one side of her. The toe-the-line, by-the-book version they knew. They hadn't seen the way she could fearlessly conquer a cliff in the North Georgia woods, the way she paddled an ocean kayak with abandon into the inky darkness of night. The way she faced risk head-on sometimes.

They saw only the Claire that had returned to Treasure Point after Justin's accident.

"I know, sir."

"You keep her safe."

Nate nodded and left the room, heading to his motorcycle, which he'd parked out front. He'd pick her up at Gemma's house and then figure out what to do.

The hum of his bike and the smoothness of the road gave him more time to think about what he wanted out of this case. Almost as much as he wanted to take drug smugglers and manufacturers off the street in general, Nate wanted to get some kind of justice for people who had been hurt by their effects. And the thing he had wanted for the entire duration of this particular case in Treasure Point was to make Claire's world safe enough that she'd be able to make the choice on her own whether or not she wanted to pursue the more risky life of adventure she'd been living in college. Yes, she'd changed, but he'd seen enough sparks of the old Claire to think that she wasn't entirely gone.

The way she'd responded to his question that night when they'd walked around to look at Christmas lights, before shots had been fired, when he'd asked what she wanted out of life…she'd responded too quickly that all she wanted was to stay in Treasure Point. Claire had been defensive to the point that Nate was almost sure she still had dreams bigger than this town, than her shop.

What about her art? Back in college, she'd talked of aiming for a gallery showing, striving to make a living from the craft she loved. Was it now just a hobby for her spare time that happened to decorate her shop? Nate would guess the latter. Making it as a professional artist took a little bit of a willingness to be reckless.

He pulled his bike in front of the O'Dells' house and waved to the other officer who drove off once Nate had reached the front porch.

"Hey." Claire grinned when she saw him, letting him into the house. "So what did they say at the meeting? Am I going to get to see you take him down? I wasn't expecting you to come back until later."

Nate had to laugh a little at her enthusiasm. He suspected she got her idea of how cases like this ended from TV. While he'd certainly take a TV-perfect finish, sometimes bringing a suspect into custody was a little messier. Lines were blurred. Good guys got shot and sometimes didn't make it.

Not something he could afford to think about right now. He had to keep his head in the game for when it was his turn to be the one chasing Brad in one way or another.

FOURTEEN

"No," he told Claire, shaking his head. "I'm not going to be part of this round of surveillance."

"What?"

He explained the chief's reasoning about cars and liability.

"But couldn't you ride with someone? It doesn't seem fair that you don't get to be part of the stakeout."

Nate just looked at her.

Understanding came quickly. "Oh. Someone has to babysit me. I forgot. Wow… I'm sorry, Nate."

"Not your fault."

"So what now?"

Nate shrugged. "I'm supposed to distract you."

Claire turned to him, eyebrows raised. "Like you're going to be able to make me forget that someone wants me dead?"

"Look, I know that's not going to happen. But sitting around staring at the walls isn't going to make this end any sooner. Maybe we drive around a little? I can take pictures and you can see if there's anything you might want to paint sometime?" He hadn't been sure if bringing up painting would bring happy emotions or sad with it, but she did smile a little.

"That might be nice, I guess. It's safe enough?"

"We're making plans spur of the moment, so there won't be any ambushes like with the Christmas lights. We won't be at any place the killer expects you to be, so nothing could have been planned ahead of time. I'll keep an eye out for tails, but yes, Claire, I think you'll be safe today. Let's go."

Claire stood, walked toward the door and started to grab her keys.

"We're taking the bike. Ready?" Nate asked Claire.

"Uh, not so much."

"You don't think she's riding your motorcycle, do you, Nate?" Gemma asked as she walked into the entryway from the kitchen. "Somehow when I think Claire, I don't think *motorcycle*."

Claire shot Gemma a look. "What's that supposed to mean?"

"Nothing besides the fact that I don't think they're your style." She held up her hands in mock surrender. "You know I love you, Claire. You're my favorite sister." Nate guessed it was some kind of joke between them since he was pretty sure they were each other's only sisters. "I just don't think it's your thing."

"I like some things that are unexpected. My love for '80s music? No one ever expects that."

Gemma laughed. "Not really the same, sis, but if you say so. Have fun." Gemma looked at Nate one more time, and Nate felt like she was sizing him up. As what, exactly, was anyone's guess.

"So you're coming?" Nate asked Claire when they were alone again.

Claire nodded. Slowly.

"You didn't tell your sister that you've ridden with me before."

"No, I didn't."

"Is there a reason for that?"

"My sister…we're close. But even with Gemma… I never told her the whole story about Savannah. College was the first time in my life I was really able to cut loose and try different things, take risks without my parents and Gemma giving me a hard time about it. I loved that life…but it was so different from what everyone expected me to be. So I kept it to myself. I didn't want to disappoint anyone. Even though I called and emailed Gemma all the time, whenever I told her what I was up to, I left that stuff out. She knew about Justin, but just that he was my boyfriend, and that he died my junior year."

"So you've let all your old hobbies go? You don't do any of it anymore?"

"Well, I still go rock climbing in Savannah sometimes. Gemma knows about that, but she only found out recently when I kept making trips to Savannah and she insisted on knowing what those were about. The rest of it…she just never knew."

"Shouldn't she?"

Claire shrugged. "Why? It's not who I am anymore."

"Isn't it?"

She glared back at him. He held up his hands in mock surrender. "You want me to leave it alone. Got it. Let's go."

They went outside and climbed on the bike. He put on his own helmet, handed her one, watched her blink back surprise. "You didn't think I was going to ask you to ride with me without a helmet, did you? Risk is fine, Claire, but not stupid choices. There is a difference." Maybe that was the problem. Rather than invite too much danger into her life, like Nate knew Justin had had a tendency to do, Claire had decided to eliminate as much risk as possible. That was no way to live. In fact, if you asked Nate, it was barely living at all.

"Where'd you get a second helmet?" she asked as she slipped it on over her wavy hair.

"I picked it up in town—the auto shop carries them."

"Where are we headed?"

"I've been doing most of my photography around town so that I could keep an eye out for suspicious activity. Since today I've basically been ordered to let the police department do surveillance, maybe we could go to the outskirts of town. I had some spots I wanted to check out as far as photography is concerned. I thought you could come along." This was a good compromise. He wouldn't be far out of town, so if something did change with Brad, he could make it back quickly, leave Claire somewhere safe and join the action.

"That sounds like fun. I could probably even show you a couple of my favorite spots to paint, in case those might translate well to another medium. It still won't make me forget someone wants me dead, but it's all we can do, I guess."

Nate decided to ignore the last part of that speech. "I don't think your painting and my photography are that similar. You're a real artist, Claire. I just dabble in pictures now and then."

"I doubt that's true."

Nate turned the key in the bike, revved the engine.

Man, he loved that sound. "You're sure you're ready?" he shouted to Claire over the noise.

"Much as I'm going to be."

Nate looked back at her, noticed she was trying to hold on to the sides of her seat. Not really a practical idea if one actually wanted to stay *on* the bike.

"You know you'll probably need to hang on to my waist if we start going too fast." She nodded but didn't move yet.

Nate took off slowly, accelerating more as they continued down the road. So far Claire seemed to be hanging on okay. Maybe she had better balance than he'd realized. Surprising since she'd confirmed what he'd suspected—that it had been almost a decade since she'd ridden on a motorcycle.

They weren't too far into the first curve, though, when he felt her arms go around his waist.

Nate smiled to himself and kept driving.

He'd heard about a place overlooking the marsh and ocean that was supposed to have an incredible view. If it panned out, he might come back another day at sunrise and try to get some pictures of the sun over the ocean. But today he wanted to go in the daylight and just see what it was like. The trail to the overlook was behind Treasure Point High School.

They kicked up dust as the road turned from concrete to dirt, then narrowed into little more than a trail. Nate followed it as far back as he dared and parked the bike. "Looks like we're going to have to walk from here," he said to Claire as they climbed off. "What did you think of the ride?"

She still hadn't stopped grinning. "It was okay."

He could get used to seeing her smile that way. Spend

a lot of years thinking up ways to put that happy look on her face.

Nate almost jumped out of his skin at the direction of his own thoughts. Was he really thinking of spending years with her? Yes, that had been some kiss the other night. But it had been for their cover, and he had *no* intention of letting it happen again. The spark between them had been too strong to ignore, but much, *much* too strong to pay attention to. Setting aside the facts and thinking of feelings could only lead to pain for both of them. They were wrong for each other, fundamentally. Claire wanted safe. Forever. And Nate wasn't going to give up his dream job for her white picket fence life.

Nate started walking, hoping to burn off some of the fidgety energy caused by thinking about that kiss. "Ready to go find this spot I've heard about?" he called back to Claire.

"Sure, let's go." She hurried along behind him.

"I think we go left here." Nate squinted at the little path between the trees. He led the way, Claire following, and made several turns before leading them right to where he'd meant to be—a small bluff that overlooked a marsh creek on the north side of Treasure Point.

He whistled. It was picture-perfect now—at sunrise, he knew it was going to be dazzling.

The water was glassy calm, the creek twisting and turning through the gold-and-green marsh. The mid-morning sun was turning everything a glowing shade of gold—everything felt warm.

Nate pulled his camera from his pack without speaking and snapped a few shots. Walked a little closer and snapped a few more. He paused once or twice to check on Claire and make sure she was okay and still with him.

She'd settled down on the ground less than ten feet away, so he went back to his camera, completely spellbound by whatever it was he was seeing here. He couldn't quite put his finger on it.

"It's incredible, isn't it?"

"It is." He exhaled, lowered his camera and just took it in, liking the way the scene somehow felt like warm honey, soothing the places inside him that were jagged and rough. He'd be coming back here again. One day, even if it wasn't soon. Because he wouldn't have time to explore any more if the case wrapped up. He'd be headed out of town as soon as it did, back to the city to find more darkness to fight against. It was a never-ending battle, one he'd always thought was worth fighting. But here, now, it was hard to picture going back to a life that lacked this…this sense of quiet. He could see why Claire liked the area. Nate sat down on the ground beside her. "Have you been here before?"

"I have. It's one of my favorite places to paint."

"I can see why. I'd love to look at your paintings of this place sometime, find out if we see it the same way."

"You claim that your photography isn't an art the same way my painting is. But you talk like you understand art, Nate."

He shook his head. Photography was a hobby, nothing more. It just happened to be serving him well at the moment during this case. "So. Tell me about growing up here." As long as they were settled on the warm earth, looking out at the creek and then the ocean on the horizon, he might as well broach the subject he'd been wondering about.

"What do you want to know?"

She'd turned to face him, and the way the sun was

hitting her blond waves made her look even more open and approachable than she usually did. Nate wondered for a minute if Claire had any idea how beautiful she was—approachable, sweet and incredibly attractive at the same time.

"I want to know the real Claire." The words were out of his mouth, hanging in the air, waiting to see what she'd do with them, before Nate had even finished the thought. It was true, 100 percent, but made him more vulnerable than he would have liked to be.

"You're the first person to ask me a question like that." She looked away from him, and Nate was relatively certain she was intentionally avoiding his eyes. Her next words were soft. "I'm just so tired of people thinking they know me. That they understand."

Not an answer, not really. But it still gave him more insight into her.

"I know how that goes." Nate told her that when his sister died, people assumed they knew how he was feeling. And they very rarely did.

She looked back at him. "I don't have an answer for you, Nate."

"Tell me this, then. Why did you leave Treasure Point for college, get into rock climbing and kayaking and all that?"

"It's funny. Gemma and I have talked about how she never felt like she measured up to me because I was the 'perfect' sister." Claire made a face to go along with the air quotes. "But I just… I wanted to be more than that, *different* than that after high school. So I used college to do the things I'd always dreamed of, as a chance to be more adventurous, really spend time outdoors and take chances. And then I...took too many chances. Too many risks."

She was talking about Justin's death. Nate had wondered if that played into this. He had no idea what to say to that, only knew that the reminder of the man who'd been his only close friend stole any other words or thoughts from his mind.

They sat in silence as the Georgia sun finished moving up in the sky until it was straight overhead. Something about the way they could be together without needing to talk made him feel even closer to her. Claire might be the last person who *should* have understood him, but oddly enough, Nate thought she probably did. Or *could* if he let his guard down as much as she'd been willing to do—something Nate wasn't willing to do right now. And maybe never would be.

Claire could have sat there with Nate all day if her stomach hadn't growled and reminded her that she hadn't eaten much breakfast that morning.

"Hungry?" He glanced over at her and grinned, the smile making him look younger than he usually did. She enjoyed seeing him like this.

"Starved."

"Let's head back, then."

They were about halfway down the trail to the motorcycle when Nate's phone rang. He stopped and pulled it out. "Hello?"

Claire stopped walking, too, and just listened. She couldn't hear the other person on the phone, but Nate's voice sounded businesslike.

"No. I didn't expect that... Okay, that changes everything. Thanks for calling. I'll be in touch."

He put the phone away and looked over at her. Claire noted that his face had gone back to the tight, brooding expression he wore more often than not.

"That was Matt. They think Brad must be on to us, because he hasn't come out of the bike shop all day."

"Did they send anyone in there to confirm that he's actually there?"

"No, they don't want to risk showing their hand. But the shop's open. He doesn't have any other employees, does he?"

"No, I don't believe so. So what happens now?"

"Nothing new. They just keep waiting. Want to head into town for some lunch?"

"That would be good."

Claire climbed on the motorcycle behind Nate with less hesitation this time. She had missed this sense of total freedom, just on the edge of being out of control, that she always felt on a motorcycle. On the back of Nate's bike, her arms wrapped around him, Claire felt brave, like someone who didn't let life happen to her, like someone who knew what she wanted and went for it.

On the back of Nate's bike, she felt like the Claire she wanted to be. Like the one she was when she was rock climbing. The version of herself she'd tried too hard to insist had died after the accident on the north Georgia cliff that neither she nor Justin had had any business trying to climb.

But maybe she was still the same Claire after all.

Claire relaxed into Nate as they tore down the road, the oak braches overhead making striking shadows that they drove in and out of. Nate must have noticed the way she'd relaxed, because he called back, "Having fun?"

"Okay, I admit I am!" she yelled.

The sensation of the motorcycle underneath her, the way she could feel it through her whole body when Nate sped up, made her want this ride never to end. Made her want to take many more like it in the future. Maybe even learn—

Her thoughts were interrupted as they suddenly swerved, tossing them left and then right, driving them off the paved road, onto the gravel. Claire's eyes widened and she felt her grip tighten. She knew enough about motorcycles to know that going off road accidentally was far from safe.

Nate knew, too, no doubt. He slammed on the brakes, but the arrested motion upset the balance of the bike even further, and the next thing Claire knew they were both on the ground, bike on top of them. The roar of the bike was replaced by haunting silence and the loud pounding of her own heart.

"Not malicious," Nate assured her. "Not any kind of setup, Claire. It was just an accident."

"An accident that almost killed us both!"

"We're okay. Not even scratched."

"But we almost weren't. I'm not riding that bike again."

"We have to get back to town. Lunch, remember?"

Claire shook her head. Nate looked at her, apparently saw how serious she was. He pulled off his helmet. "Claire. The bike is fine. We are fine. The road is fine."

"I'm not getting back on."

He stared at her for another minute. Then calmly set his helmet down. "Fine. We'll walk."

They started walking. "If it's okay with you, I'd rather just go back to Gemma's for lunch," she said. "Not go out anywhere."

"That's fine."

What was he thinking right now? Claire wished she knew. Although maybe not, since she assumed one of his feelings was disappointment. The way he'd bantered with her earlier that day, when Gemma had teased her about riding a motorcycle…he remembered all the time they'd spent together years ago. Claire knew that playing it safe, running her coffee shop, painting on the side and not doing anything else, kept the people in town happy with her. Gemma thought nothing of it since she didn't know much about those college years, about the way Claire had almost changed and then gone immediately back to what was familiar and comfortable.

But Nate was likely disappointed. And if she was honest with herself…so was Claire.

They ate lunch quietly. Gemma didn't ask any questions.

"If you don't mind," Nate said afterward, "I'd like to go back and get my bike. I'm not comfortable leaving it there."

"Sure," Claire said. "We can take my car. Then you can follow me back here. That will keep us safe enough, right?"

Safe. There was that word again. When was Claire going to realize that it didn't mean what she wanted it to mean? *Safe* was never a guarantee. Never the only end goal.

"Yes," he said, because he thought they would be safe, and because he knew she needed to hear it.

"I'm ready when you are." She offered him a small smile. "You can even drive."

"Let's go, then."

They walked to her car in silence, still didn't talk as they climbed in.

As soon as Claire shut the door, she turned to him. "I'm sorry."

"You don't have to be."

"I was scared. And I meant what I said. I don't want to ride it again. But I shouldn't have been quite so…"

"It's okay, Claire. Really."

"Okay."

He could tell she didn't believe him that it was okay, but it was. Nate couldn't say he hadn't been disappointed, as he had felt like he'd finally made progress helping Claire be who she really was—only to cause a setback himself by not noticing the obstacle in the road in time to avoid it. Although, really, he'd done the best he could. The shoe in the road could have flipped the motorcycle if he hadn't swerved out of the way.

They were passing through town, not far from the road they needed to take, when something caught Nate's eye.

"Is that…" he said slowly, not believing his eyes at first. "Look to the right for me—is that Brad? I've only seen pictures of him so far."

"Where?"

"The parking lot by the grocery store." As he spoke, he pulled into a different parking lot across the street. They weren't so close that Brad would be able to see who was in the car without obviously squinting, but close enough they could watch his movements.

"I don't see any of the police cars."

"They're bound to have it under control," Nate said, but wasn't sure if he believed it. Brad looked around like he expected to be watched. Got into his car.

And started driving.

Nate felt his shoulders tense, felt his focus sharpen as he readied for the chase…the chase he really shouldn't take place in…

"Go! Don't lose him!"

Who was the professional here? Nate appreciated her enthusiasm, though. He reversed slowly and followed the car at a decent distance.

"Get your phone out, Claire. Call the station and tell them what we're doing." The chief would be angry that they had gotten involved, but Nate hadn't seen any other choices. Brad was leaving town, and if he'd been spooked, he might not come back. Nate wasn't going to lose eighteen months of work because he didn't have an appropriate vehicle for a chase.

There appeared to be one other person in the car, in the passenger seat, but Nate couldn't tell much about the person—tall, that was all he could see.

Maybe Jesse Carson? Tony's brother? It was a guess, but not necessarily a bad one.

They followed the car out of town and then turned south down the highway. Nate kept enough distance that he shouldn't appear as an obvious tail. Then again, Claire's Mini Cooper didn't exactly lend itself to blending in.

Brad turned onto a back road. And another, this one dirt.

"He's on to us. Knows we're tailing him." Nate knew he'd almost growled the words, didn't love the fact that Claire was seeing him like this, but he couldn't hide his frustration. He couldn't stop following the car, either. Even if Brad was leading them into a trap, they still needed eyes on his location or they risked losing him entirely.

Nate gripped the steering wheel as hard as he could, released his grip and squeezed again.

"Why do you think so? What's wrong?"

The road they were on seemed to dead-end up ahead… yet as they got closer, Nate could see that wasn't entirely true. There was a hard T-shaped turn at a grove of pine trees. The car they were following turned right and Nate swung his wheel to follow, then pressed the gas a little bit. If Brad was already on to them, he might as well drop all pretense and try to get as close—

The heavy thud of metal on metal was followed instantly by his car screeching towards a halt.

The steering wheel refused to move—everything was locked—and the car pulled hard to the left and lurched to a stop. Nate had heard of this happening to a friend before when a strut rod bushing hadn't been tightened all the way. In his friend's case, it had been an accident, but Nate was almost sure Claire's car had been tampered with. That would have caused car to break down like this not long into the drive. Brad wouldn't have been able to predict the exact location of their breakdown, but he would have known that a little driving would wiggle the part off and cause this malfunction before too much time had passed.

The car was undrivable. And they were stuck in the woods with several men who were likely killers.

"What's going on?" There was no hint of teasing in her voice now, only a gravity that said she realized the seriousness of the situation.

"Not sure."

There were no other cars on the road—either this was a huge coincidence or a fantastic setup. Even the car they were following was out of sight. Chills ran down Nate's arms, made his hair stand on end. If this had all been orchestrated, they could be in danger.

Stay in the car or move?

"Nate."

"Sit tight, Claire. Call 911 again and tell them where we are. Hopefully someone is close since you updated them earlier." He opened his door without waiting for her reply and stepped outside. The air was warmer today than it had been the last few days—he didn't really need the jacket he'd brought with him and tossed in the back. Weird weather for December. It probably meant that a storm was coming soon.

The wind through the pines whistled slightly, an eerie noise that made the goose bumps on his arms rise even more. He shivered, then turned back to the car. He heard nothing but the wind, saw no evidence of any people around at all.

He'd just opened the door when he caught sight of Brad's car heading straight toward them.

"Get out of the car," Nate ordered.

She obeyed without complaint but then looked at him, eyebrows raised. She slid her phone, still connected to the 911 operator per their instructions, into her pocket. "Okay, and now?"

The approaching car jerked to the side of the road.

"Now run."

The first gunshots peppered the ground next to Claire's Mini Cooper right where she'd been standing seconds before. "Into the pines!" Nate yelled and waited for her to pass him.

"Where?" she yelled from the front.

"As deep as you can go for as long as you can go!"

Their footsteps pounded the ground scattered with

pine needles and dirt, and the gunshots kept coming. Neither of them had been hit yet, though.

For now, all they could do was keep running. And hope the shooters ran out of ammo.

FIFTEEN

Finally, what felt like hours later, long minutes of silence confirmed that whoever had been shooting at them had given up.

"Could they be moving closer?" Claire whispered from where she sat, so close to Nate he could almost feel her breath on his face.

"I don't think so," he answered slowly, not wanting to be too optimistic, even though he genuinely thought that they were in the clear for now.

"How do you know?"

"I think I heard the car drive away."

"Couldn't it have been another car?"

"I guess so." Nate looked at her, long and hard, searching her eyes.

"What?"

"I need to go check it out."

He watched Claire steel herself.

"Okay. Go. Be careful."

"I will be. You, too. If anyone approaches who isn't me, run. I should be less than five minutes."

"Okay."

He looked back one time, confirmed that she was still

okay, and then trekked out of the woods far enough to assure himself that their attackers were gone.

He also heard sirens. Backup. "You can come out, Claire," he called, and she emerged from the woods. She stayed back as he moved forward and spoke with the newly arrived officers. When the conversation was over, he jogged over to give her the update.

"They're going to do a full sweep of your car to make sure there's nothing wrong—bombs, anything like that. For now, Officer Hitchcock is going to give you a ride home. Matt is off duty and waiting there. Stay with him."

Nate hadn't wanted to leave Claire, but he knew that after they finished securing the crime scene, he would need to go to the police department to tell them everything that had happened. He'd also need to call Wade to make a full report. Being shot at was bad—Nate hated that Claire'd had to experience that again—but at least it was something Nate was used to. Bullets tended to fly between groups in the drug world, and Nate had been literally caught in the crossfire once a few years back. He had the scar on his right shoulder to prove it.

But as bad as the shooting had been, it was the planning behind it, the way that Brad and the other man appeared to have led them out of town intentionally, that concerned him.

"Found something."

One of the officers pulled a note from underneath the windshield wipers of Claire's car. It was folded so small Nate had missed it.

GIVE UP THE ACT, TORRES. WE KNOW WHO YOU ARE.

And his cover was officially blown.

"Agent Torres."

The chief motioned to him from several squad cars away. "We need to talk. Come down to the station with me."

Nate climbed in.

The chief didn't say much on the drive. "I don't like to talk business when I'm driving," he explained. "I'd rather keep my eyes open for troublemakers."

Nate understood that. Considering the afternoon he'd had, he welcomed the silence.

Once they arrived at the police department, Nate filled the chief in on what had happened. "I'm sorry if you felt I interfered with your officers' surveillance, sir. It was my intention to tail Brad and give updates on his location until your officers could take over. I certainly never thought Claire would be in physical danger or I wouldn't have gone."

"I'm not sure you *were* thinking, other than wanting to take this guy down."

"Be that as it may, I've been on this case for too long to quit on it now. Protecting Claire is important, but so is solving this."

"You need someone else to be put on security detail for her? I might be able to spare a man for a few days. If you think you can wrap this up that quickly."

"I think it might be necessary. I'm close. So close. Even if they know who I am now, I've been tracking the Carsons for months. I know Jesse's habits, hangouts... I'm ready for this."

"Starting tomorrow? I can't spare a guy until eleven, but you could leave Claire after that."

Nate hesitated, unsure whether he was thinking with

his heart or his head. Or for that matter, which he should listen to. "Tomorrow's Christmas Eve. Let me tell her the change of plans. But yes. Eleven o'clock, your guy can take over." He needed to focus on the case rather than on Claire, even if part of him rebelled at the idea.

"Sounds like a plan."

"Thank you, sir. I've appreciated your department's help."

"Of course. You stay safe, Torres."

It was the first time the chief had called him by only his last name—something he'd noticed the older man only did when he really liked someone. Nate grinned for a second as he walked out the door.

He walked across town to where he and Claire had left the motorcycle earlier, then climbed onto his bike and set a course for the O'Dells' house. Thoughts of telling Claire he was stepping away from her protection detail haunted him as he drove.

Nate pressed the gas a little harder, burned up the road a little louder. After the action today, he felt urgency pressing in on him to bring this case to a close. Statistics would catch up to Claire eventually, and as many times as she'd almost been killed, Nate wasn't happy with that idea at all. He needed her to stay safe, and that wouldn't happen until this whole investigation came to an end. They were getting closer, at least. Evidence had confirmed that Trace Johnson had killed Jenni because of his ties to the drug ring—a large sum of money deposited into his account immediately after the murder had taken place. But he was just a man they were using to do their dirty work. Not the man they were ultimately after.

It was time to take the bad guys down and hope that one of the men they were already aware of was the head of the organization. It seemed likely. And Nate was getting more and more sure that it was Brad.

Help me out, God. This is getting messier by the minute and I can't figure out half of what I should be doing.

He pulled into the O'Dells' driveway and wasted no time parking his bike and making his way to the entrance.

Claire opened the door. Nate actually blinked when he saw her—somehow she'd gotten more beautiful than earlier.

"Hey. I made cookies if you want to have some with your coffee."

Cookies and coffee. It felt so…normal. Like tomorrow he wasn't going to try to go catch the head of a drug ring. For a moment, he felt like an average man, with an average job, just enjoying the company of a woman who fascinated and intrigued him.

And for this one evening, he was going to let himself ignore all the reasons that wasn't true.

She moved to the kitchen, which was empty, and started setting out plates for them.

"Where are Gemma and Matt? You're not alone, right?" Panic started to creep over him, but it disappeared as soon as she shook her head.

"No, they're just upstairs watching a movie."

Nate frowned. Not a lot better. He would rather have had someone physically by Claire's side the entire time he'd been gone.

"It's fine, Nate," she said in response to his expression, which he hadn't realized she'd be able to read. Surely he hadn't gotten that transparent—talk about something that was a disadvantage in undercover work. But how could she read him so well?

"You were shot at today," he said.

"And I'm fine."

"But—"

She handed him a plate with a couple of delicious-looking cookies on it and a mug of coffee. "Here, let's sit down and eat. How did it go with the police?"

"It went well. Really well." They settled down on the couch together.

"Claire…after tomorrow morning, the Treasure Point Police Department is going to take over your protective detail for the time being."

So much for being a normal guy for the evening. He'd brought up work after less than five minutes.

She turned toward him. Was that hurt in her eyes? Confusion? Nate saw something but couldn't quite identify it.

"Okay."

"You don't want to know why?"

She shook her head. "I'm sure you have your reasons. So what's next for you after this?" Claire shifted on the couch to face him. "I know you're hoping this case will wrap up soon."

"I don't know." And he didn't. The last time he'd heard from Wade, his boss had hinted at another deep cover assignment possibility. A big one. Usually that would have piqued Nate's interest, but now…

His heart wasn't in it. But how could he not do it? This was the job he'd always wanted. It was why he woke up every morning and faced life without his sister.

Finding justice was his purpose. He couldn't even picture God having another one for him. But admittedly… Nate had never asked.

"I'm not sure exactly," he started again. "Something back in Atlanta."

"Do you miss the city?"

He studied Claire's face. She was too cheery, like she was holding back how she really felt, trying to mask emotions she didn't want him to see.

Nate shrugged. "It's okay. Your town has its charms."

"Yeah…" Her voice trailed off. She looked uncertain.

"Do you think you'll stay in Treasure Point forever?" Nate asked to turn the focus off himself.

"Probably."

"But is that really what you want?"

Claire frowned. "I'm…not sure."

If he guessed right, Claire was afraid to leave Treasure Point. It was so closely tied to her hesitancy to be the real Claire rather than this version of herself the town seemed to expect that Nate wasn't sure he could untangle her motivations enough to figure out which was which.

"You'd be fine leaving or staying, Claire. You're an amazing woman." All of it true. All of it also designed to push this conversation about jobs, moving and the case back, leave reality for another night. They'd had enough of reality in the form of flying bullets today. This wasn't what they needed tonight, and Nate could feel the tension building enough to know that if he didn't redirect this conversation soon, tonight wasn't going to end well.

As it was, she accepted the redirection. "Want to watch a movie down here?"

"Sure. Something Christmassy," he said, surprising himself.

She came back with a movie, handed him the case while she put the DVD in.

"John Wayne?" Nate asked, laughing. "John Wayne has a Christmas movie?"

"*Donovan's Reef* is technically a Christmas movie. It takes place at Christmas and it has one of the most meaningful Christmas plays I've ever seen."

"I guess I'm going to have to watch it to believe it."

Claire sat down beside him, and Nate lifted an arm to the back of the couch. She snuggled into his side, eventually laying her head against his shoulder as they watched the movie until later in the night.

Nate soaked in every minute of it. He felt almost like tonight was a pleasant break, the eye of the storm.

The whole case, her safety, everything could very well explode tomorrow. He didn't know. There were no guarantees. But for tonight, he'd sit here with her, watching this Christmas movie, and be thankful for whatever short time they had.

Before tomorrow came and Nate started putting distance between them again. Distance they both needed if they were going to move on in their lives the way they'd planned.

"Can I come in?" Gemma's soft knock on Claire's door after they'd all gone to bed surprised her, so she wasted no time in getting up and opening the door.

"Is everything okay?" Claire asked.

Her sister stood in her pj's and a bathrobe. "Everything's as okay as it's been, I guess. I just… Every time there's been another attack and I've come so close to losing you, I think about all the things I wish I'd done differently, all the ways we could have been closer." Gemma shrugged. "You were there for me when I went through everything earlier this year, even when I didn't really want you to be." She made a face. "But I don't feel like I've been there for you."

"You've got Matt now. I know you're busy and have a lot on your mind. Your husband, the museum…and… unless I miss my guess…"

Her eyes dropped to her sister's stomach.

Gemma's eyes widened. "How did you…?"

"You haven't had coffee in the last week, even though you've poured it for me. I've been wrapped up in my own life, too, sis, but I'm not dumb."

Gemma smiled. "It's really early. Matt's the only one who knows."

"I'm so excited for you." And she was.

But the tangles in her mind just grew tighter, and Claire started to doubt even more whether she could figure this all out. The irony made Claire smile a little. Gemma had always referred to Claire as the perfect sister. Yet here they were, and Gemma had a perfect little family, a job she loved, a home…

Claire had a shop that didn't truly fulfill her—and that had been all but destroyed through the attacks— and a crush on a man who could never possibly return the feelings.

"So are you going to tell me why you look so serious?" Gemma asked. "Something besides the case is bothering you, isn't it?

Claire thought about brushing Gemma off, keeping the focus on her sister. But… Gemma had shared with her. Maybe Claire should take the next step to making the two of them close again, like they'd been before.

"It's Nate. It's…complicated. And I told myself not to let my heart get involved, but…"

"Really? You've known him for a week."

Claire shook her head, watched Gemma's eyes widen. "What?" Gemma asked.

"There's a lot you don't know about when I was in college."

"What does that have to do with Nate?"

Claire told her the details she didn't know about Justin—Gemma had known she'd had a boyfriend, just not the specifics—Nate and Katie, about the things they'd done together, the adventures they'd had. She told Gemma the truth, that she'd been drawn only to Justin, but that Nate had been a good friend.

"Justin…when he went to grad school and our relationship became long-distance, I started to feel like I was losing him. I went up to visit, found him out with another girl. It was pretty much exactly what I'd been worried about—that I was too small-town for him, not exciting or glamorous enough to hold his attention. He promised it wouldn't happen again, it was just a mistake, so I gave him another chance and tried to come up more on the weekends to spend time with him.

"Things seemed okay for a month or two. We were spending a lot of time rock climbing…but then Justin chose a place to climb that was beyond our skill level. At first I said no, but when I saw how disappointed he was, I changed my mind. I didn't want him to think that I was holding him back. So I went anyway. And… and he died."

"I remember when that happened. I just didn't know you were with him when he fell. That was your junior year?"

Claire nodded. "My grades took a hit—it was hard to concentrate in class after that. I pulled it back together for senior year, but by then I mostly just wanted to be done with classes so I could come home."

"So you came back to town, went back to your fall-back plan in your mind, and stopped taking chances. Am I right?" Gemma read the situation well.

"Yes."

"And Nate is the only one who knows both versions of Claire. The one who does love Treasure Point, but also the one who longs for adventure."

Claire nodded slowly, glad it was so clear to her sister.

"So…maybe this is something you should give a chance. He knows you, Claire. And you don't let very many people get to know you that way. Nate must be special."

"He can't stay here in Treasure Point, Gemma. And I've tried long-distance before. It doesn't work, not for me."

"Could you go to Atlanta? Sell the coffee shop building to someone here in town once it's repaired and use the money to get yourself started, maybe check out the Atlanta art scene, sell some paintings? You do have an unused art minor just collecting dust, if I'm not mistaken."

"I don't know." Claire dropped her head into her hands. Another thing that needed to factor into Claire's decision was Gemma's baby. Claire's roots here in Treasure Point would be spreading even wider and deeper once Gemma started her family. Could she really leave her little niece or nephew?

Her mind kept going in circles. She shook her head, hoping somehow that the physical motion could clear the imaginary webs inside it.

"Have you talked to God about this at all, Claire?"

The words fell on her mind with a thud, accompanied by an empty feeling in her stomach as Claire tried to remember the last time she'd asked God anything...

Even this entire Christmas season, she'd been too busy for Him. Before the threats against her had started she'd been busy with her shop, with her plans for the season. And since her life had been in danger, Claire was pretty sure she'd sent up a few prayers begging for safety, or for wisdom in figuring out who was behind everything.

But actually talked to God, like she expected Him to listen? Spend time with Him? Spend this season celebrating His birth and what it meant for her life, maybe ask Him what it *did* mean for her life, how He wanted her to use the years she'd been given by Him?

Not even once.

God, I am so sorry. Forgive me for so completely cutting You out of my life. Is it too late to ask what You want for me? Too late to tell You that I want to have a real relationship with You?

"It's late. I'm going to head back to bed." Gemma reached out for a hug. "But I love you. I'm sorry we've drifted apart a little. We won't let that happen again."

It seemed Claire had a habit of letting relationships lapse like that. She was thankful for her sister's willingness to do better, thankful for God's grace to allow her to start fresh.

She hugged her sister back, then shut the door behind her.

Claire climbed into bed, closed her eyes, and smiled a little as she drifted off to sleep.

Here's to new beginnings...

SIXTEEN

Claire had slept better than expected after the events of the day before. When she went down the stairs the next morning, her sister had coffee going already. Except now she had another pot—Claire assumed decaf, now that her secret was out and she wasn't giving herself away.

"Good morning. Merry Christmas Eve." Claire offered Gemma a smile.

"Morning and Merry Christmas Eve to you, too. I'm sorry everything's so crazy in your life around the holidays. I know how much you love Christmas."

Claire shrugged. "It's okay. It's showing me what's important, I guess. Being alive and having people I care about."

"That's a good response, I think. What are you doing today?"

"I don't know." Claire sighed. "Nate is coming by this morning. I think he's saying goodbye, essentially."

"What do you mean?"

"He needs to focus on the case, and babysitting me is getting in the way of that. I get the impression he thinks he has enough to wrap it up soon. The chief will be sending an officer over to keep an eye on me. So Nate and

I are spending the morning together, sort of a 'farewell to an old friend' thing, and then he's gone."

"But not gone from town."

"Not yet. But he will be as soon as he gets the drug smugglers in jail."

Neither sister said anything. Claire appreciated Gemma's silence. The ache in her heart at going back to life without Nate…it wasn't something she'd expected. She didn't understand it. And she definitely didn't want to talk about it.

"I have an idea for what you can do, if you want to hear about it," Gemma said a minute later.

"Sure."

There was a knock on the door just then. "I guess he's coming earlier than I thought," Claire said.

Gemma moved toward it, but Claire held up a hand to stop her. "I'll get it. Don't you need to sit down or something?"

Gemma laughed. "I'm not expecting the baby to come today, Claire. I'm not an invalid yet." But she made no move to stop Claire from heading to the entryway.

Claire opened the door, looking up at Nate, who was somehow more handsome today than yesterday. His attire was the same, all black, but something about his face was lighter today. Maybe it was his eyes.

And the smile lines around them—he seemed less like he was carrying the weight of the entire world on his shoulders, more like he had hope for this case, for all the others.

"Good morning," she said.

"Good morning. Is there an extra cup of coffee around here?" he asked as Claire stepped aside to let him in the house.

"I think we could find one," Claire teased. She could hear Gemma pouring it in the kitchen right now. "Especially since my sister's not drinking real coffee anymore."

"What?"

Claire glanced over at Gemma, who nodded her permission.

"She's going to have a baby."

He looked over at Gemma, who Claire thought looked even more glowing today than yesterday, and smiled at her. "Congratulations!"

"Thank you." Gemma rested one hand on her still-flat stomach. "We're really excited." She handed Nate the coffee and he took it, glancing over at Claire as he took a sip.

"I was just telling Claire that I had an idea for what you could do this morning if you don't have plans."

"I don't have plans for this morning," Nate confirmed.

"And this afternoon?"

"I'm going to be working on the case, trying to connect the dots, see if I can figure out where the group's headquarters is and take them all into custody."

Claire hadn't thought of them having a headquarters, beyond the boats where they'd apparently had several meetings. But if they were manufacturing the drug, then Nate did have a point. There had to be some kind of headquarters around Treasure Point. Where, though? Claire felt like she should be able to come up with the answer, point him in the right direction. After all, she knew this place like the back of her hand, or better than that. She knew it like her cinnamon roll recipe. Like her paint box.

But the answer seemed just out of reach.

"Well, my idea," Gemma continued, "was for you to come to work with me today."

"To the museum?" Claire couldn't imagine what they would do there since it was still under construction and not set to open for another few months. Her sister was in charge of marketing, publicity, and some other details of the museum. Her job had expanded since she'd taken it because she was so good at what she did.

"Yeah, we've gotten a couple of exhibits set up. The main ones are still being worked on, of course, but like I said, we have a couple that are interesting, and I thought Nate might enjoy seeing them." She gave a pointed look to Claire. "It's important to understand history, you know. People's roots?"

Yes, yes, she understood the double meaning there. What was it about sisters that made them lose the ability to be subtle?

She looked over at Nate. "What do you think?"

To her surprise, he was nodding. "I think that's a good idea."

"Really?"

"Learning more about the area can only be a good thing." He looked over at Gemma. "Thanks for the invitation. Should we meet you there, or…?"

Gemma glanced at her watch. "I'm going to leave in about half an hour. Why don't you plan to meet me about a half an hour later, around nine?"

"We'll be there."

Gemma left the room, and Claire and Nate were alone.

They drank their coffee mostly in silence, each of them stealing glances at the other occasionally and then looking down at their coffee when they were caught.

Gemma headed out, reminding them to follow her in half an hour.

Claire still didn't know what she felt for this man, and she certainly didn't know that it was a good idea to try for any kind of relationship…but if he really was going to be back out of her life within a matter of days, it was important to her to memorize the line of his jaw, the way his brown eyes were so dark and always so full of meaning.

She'd meant to never risk her heart again.

But as she looked at him, she realized that maybe her efforts had been fruitless.

At least she hadn't said anything. She'd betrayed herself with how she'd responded to that kiss in the marsh. And he might have, too. Claire wasn't sure. But as long as neither of them said anything…they could still take the safe option of letting their attraction die out on its own.

She needed to get out of this house, get some air. Claire glanced at her watch. Close enough to time. "Should we head to the museum?"

Nate nodded. "Yeah. Let's go."

So this was the way their friendship was going to end. Not with a blowup, or a foolish plan to date and then realizing it would never work. It was just going to…fizzle.

There'd be no risk involved this way, but no real reward either. Wasn't that what Claire wanted?

They drove to the museum in Claire's car. Nate had offered his bike, but she intended to keep her promise about never riding it again. Never riding a motorcycle again *at all*. The road to the Hamilton Estate, a former plantation which the widow Hamilton had donated to the town to use for the museum, curved through a huge row of live oak trees whose branches stretched over the road. Coming back here to this historical part of Treasure Point always felt a little bit to Claire like going back in time, to another era and almost another place entirely.

The scene in front of her looked nothing like it had the last time she'd been out here. That had been not long after Gemma had gotten the job doing the museum's marketing. The museum's main building was a replica of the Hamilton House, which had stood almost on the same spot for over a century until it had burned down a few years back. It would be a nod to Treasure Point's history in several areas, but especially pirate history. This corner of Georgia had many stories about pirates. Some of the more fantastical ones that included Blackbeard having a love interest who lived in the area had turned out to be true. The historical society was hoping that the museum would make the town proud of who they were and that it would also garner business from the tourists who came through, as well as from residents of nearby towns like Savannah and Brunswick who enjoyed history.

The last time Claire had seen the museum, it had been a construction site, with the beams and framing just beginning to go up. Now it looked like a grand plantation-style house, with columns, sparkling windows and a gracious front porch.

It looked exactly as it should, just like Gemma had described. And much like the Hamilton House must have looked before it had fallen into disrepair in the last few years before its destruction.

"This is a museum?" Nate asked when they'd parked the car.

Claire nodded and then explained museum's background and area of focus.

"Pirates, huh? Interesting. And here we are looking for almost the same thing, just a different kind of modern-day pirate."

Claire didn't know why, but his observation stuck with her through their entire tour of the museum. She thought about it as they passed sections that were still under construction, clear plastic hanging down over what would be displays, or over sections of the walls that weren't quite finished, and she thought about it in the finished areas of the museum too, where plaques explaining the historical significance of items were already posted.

But it was in front of the First Pirates in Treasure Point display that his idea echoed the loudest in her head as her gaze fixed on a particular place along the model of the coast.

The old lighthouse.

She turned to Gemma first. "I'm sorry, but we have to go."

Her sister looked at her in confusion until Claire glanced at Nate and finished explaining. "The old lighthouse. It's very near Hurricane Edges, where that boat came past us. What if that's where they were headed?"

Understanding dawned in Nate's eyes and he nodded. "What if that's the headquarters?"

It would be so easy for Claire to take one of Matt's kayaks out in the general direction of the lighthouse, just to see if their suspicions were correct. It would be so, so easy...and the idea was incredibly tempting. This case had been shadowing her all this time, and now that it was nearly over, she wanted to see how it would end.

It wasn't a smart idea—if her life were a movie, this

would be the part where everyone yelled at the main character, "Don't do it!"

The old Claire would have done it. She'd have been bold, fearless. Daring. All the things that the new Claire wasn't.

Which was why she didn't.

She'd driven Nate back to the house, where he'd picked up his bike and then ridden off to investigate the lead. And Claire had stayed at home, like a good girl, and waited to hear any updates. So far, there had been nothing.

At least she wasn't there alone. Gemma had come home for lunch and announced that she'd already completed all the work she needed to for the day, so she would be spending the afternoon with her sister.

With the museum's opening fast approaching, Claire was sure there was plenty of work for Gemma to be doing...but she appreciated her sister's determination to keep her company until this whole ordeal was over.

"I want to go shopping," Gemma came in and announced.

"Where?"

"Savannah. I want to go to the Babies"R"Us store there and just look around," Gemma admitted. She laughed. "I'm excited."

"Let's do it," Claire said with determination. "The officer will have to come with us."

"I'm not even sure which officer it is. I did see his car pull up, though, before Nate left."

Odd that he hadn't come in to check on them. Usually if an officer was stationed there, he'd been knocking at least now and then and checking on them face-to-face.

"Run upstairs and grab your purse," Claire said. "I'll

go tell the officer our plans." Gemma disappeared up the stairs while Claire headed to the door, trying to swallow down the bad feeling that something was about to go wrong.

The door was open, the sunshine outside blocked by the shadows of two men in the doorway, advancing too quickly to slam the door shut on them. Had they seen Gemma? Claire hoped not.

There was Brad, along with another man Claire recognized from pictures Nate had showed her as Jesse Carson—likely the man who had attacked her in the square.

It happened too fast to react at all. Fast and in slow motion at the same time, like a terrible nightmare Claire couldn't escape from.

Carson had a gun, aimed directly at her. And then he looked at Brad for direction.

He looked at *Brad*.

Brad was in charge?

Claire's views of Treasure Point, of people…everything shifted. There really were no guarantees. Nothing, no one, was ever 100 percent safe.

"You're coming with us," Brad told her. "We'll take care of you and that GBI agent at the same time."

Claire heard a soft gasp behind her. Gemma!

"You won't get Nate," Claire said with confidence, speaking loudly to cover any sound that Gemma might make. Bad enough that these men had been terrorizing her for the past week. She would *not* let them hurt her little sister, or risk the niece or nephew on the way. She angled her hands behind her back, using her fingers to signal "9," then "1" and then "1" again, hoping her sister would get the message to go upstairs and call the police.

"We won't even have to try," Brad sneered. "We'll let him know we have you, and he'll come right to us."

Jesse stepped inside, around Claire, and stood behind her, then shoved her forward with the butt of the gun. Claire swallowed hard, because she knew they were right.

Nate would be coming for her. And then Brad would waste no time in killing both of them.

"She's gone."

Gemma's shaky voice on the phone shot an extra burst through Nate's already adrenaline-overloaded veins.

"What? How?"

"I don't know. I'm afraid to go outside to see what happened to the officer who was watching the house. I can see that the car is still there, but...she opened the door, planning to tell the officer that we wanted him to take us to Savannah to go shopping." Gemma sniffed. "It was my idea. I really thought we'd be safer getting out of town."

"Who took Claire?"

"Brad Reid and another guy. Tall, heavy-set, dark hair, medium skin."

"Jesse Carson." Nate could have hit something.

"They took her," Gemma repeated.

"Call Matt. Let the chief know."

"I already did. They're starting to search now. They've got a plan to canvass the entire town with some kind of grid."

Good. He'd let them handle that, and he'd head to the places that he most expected Claire to be held hostage.

The problem was deciding between his options. Should he head to the lighthouse, where he'd been planning to search? Or check out Brad's residence, or Jesse's hotel room? Nate thought they had enough probable cause to get a warrant. What he didn't know was where they'd be more likely to keep her.

His mind kept coming back to the lighthouse. They didn't know for sure that it was the headquarters, but it seemed like a good option. And if Brad and Jesse knew the police were on to them, they wouldn't hide out in places where they thought the police would look, like their residences.

It was where Nate had been planning to head soon. What were the chances that was where Claire was being held?

Assuming she was being held at all and not...

He couldn't think of that, couldn't think of her being lifeless. It couldn't be too late. *God, please, don't let it be. Keep her safe. I have to believe that You are watching over her so I can keep going.*

Hands gripping the handlebars of his motorcycle, Nate thought of nothing but rescuing Claire. Solving the case? That would be a nice bonus. But right now he didn't care whose cover was blown, whose plans were thrown off. All he wanted was to get to Claire before anything happened that he couldn't fix.

He gunned the engine even harder, speeding toward the lighthouse. He hadn't gotten to tell her how he felt yet. Hadn't gotten to tell her that when they'd kissed, something inside him had shifted. That was when he'd stopped seeing her as his friend's former girlfriend, an old acquaintance...

And started seeing her as the only woman he could picture settling down with. Or better yet, not settling down with—going on adventures with as long as they could, up until and past when they were old and gray and all their peers had given up travel and risk for the rocking chair life.

He knew one thing, though. Clearer than he'd known much of anything. He was tired of the undercover life. Tired of never having a real home, of never being able to connect with anyone because he had a cover to maintain. It was a useful existence, doing valuable work, but it wasn't what he wanted anymore. Surely there was some middle ground where he could keep working for the GBI, keep fighting crime in the way that was so important to him, and still manage to put together a life with someone. That was what he wanted.

And he wanted it with Claire.

He rounded the bend in the road that he knew meant he was almost to the lighthouse. He parked his bike there, under the shade of some trees, so he could walk up to the structure without making so much noise.

Nate climbed from the bike and hesitated, realizing he should have told Gemma where he was planning to head so she could pass it on to Matt and the other officers. He was so used to being undercover on his own that working with other law enforcement officers, as part of a team still wasn't second nature to him. Nate pulled his phone out of his pocket, dialed the police department.

Nothing. No signal.

He stood by the motorcycle for a second. Even if Claire was being held here, it wouldn't do her any good for him to intervene if he couldn't pull this off on his own. Then again, the drive into town took a good ten minutes. Could he live with himself if Claire didn't make it because he'd been twenty minutes late?

Absolutely not. He'd go in alone.

He approached the lighthouse as quietly as possible. It stood near the water in a clearing. The structure was at least fifty feet tall, Nate would guess, and beside it was an old cottage with boarded-up windows, sprayed in multiple places with graffiti.

As soon as Nate approached, the door to the lighthouse opened. Brad Reid stepped out, a rifle swung over his back.

Nate wished he could get his hands on that gun, check the ballistics against the slugs that had been found in Claire's shop. He was almost certain they'd be a match. So *Brad* had been the one to pull the trigger the night they'd looked at Christmas lights.

Nate hadn't talked to the man much, though he'd been in his shop at least once since he'd made it a point to go in all the shops in town.

But never would he have guessed him capable of this. Every year he worked this job, people surprised him more. And not in a good way.

"Well. I was just coming to look for you to bring you here. I guess you saved me the trouble. Claire Phillips is up in the top of the lighthouse." Brad looked at Nate, smiled a slow smile. "I could kill you here. But I think I'll take you upstairs. I want you to have to watch her die—to know that you failed to save her. It's the least punishment you deserve for everything you destroyed for me."

"We're stopping you from distributing a dangerous drug that never should have been invented, much less taken to the streets. Am I supposed to feel guilty for getting in the way of that?"

Brad shook his head. "People make their own choices. All I'm doing is giving them an option."

The words were sick. Evil.

A jab in his back made Nate spin around. Jesse Carson. And a large revolver.

"You're still working with him after what he did to your brother?" Nate guessed at the details of that. Guessed correctly judging by the look Jesse shot at Brad. But he said nothing, just shoved Nate up the steps.

"Keep going. No need to stall. Help isn't coming."

"There's no cell signal out here," Brad added. "You didn't think we chose this location by chance, did you?"

"You operate from here?"

"Not here," Brad scoffed. "Enough teenagers still break into the lighthouse. That wouldn't be smart. But the boarded-up cottage at the base of it is a whole different story."

"That's your lab."

Brad grinned. "Clever, yes? Absolutely no ties to me if it ever was discovered."

Except his DNA, fingerprints and all of that. If Nate could get out of this alive, they'd have more than enough to bust him. If. *If.*

"Stop thinking about what you'll do if you escape." Brad laughed, apparently having read the look on his face. "It's over." Brad's mouth spread out in an evil grin. "We've won."

Nate knew better than to believe that. No matter how much it felt that way on occasion, when heartbreak happened, and people killed each other, and drugs destroyed lives…it wasn't true. Evil was present, yes. Nate spent his days fighting it, all too aware of its presence. But it didn't win. Hope—God's hope—was just as real and far more powerful. Maybe it was time he quit blocking that out and admitted that the truth was more complicated, that life wasn't all joy but also wasn't all sadness.

"You haven't won."

"Let's take him upstairs. I'm tired of hearing him talk," Brad directed Jesse. Jesse shoved the gun deeper between Nate's shoulder blades. He sure hoped Jesse didn't slip with that thing.

As he kept taking steps up the stairs, Nate found himself drawn to pray for Claire. That she would be brave. Take risks. It was the opposite of what he wanted to pray, which was for her safety, her protection...but it was such a strong feeling that Nate prayed anyway, even as they shoved him to the top of the landing and reached the heavy door that Claire was likely behind right now, possibly paralyzed with fear. She'd worked so hard to stay out of situations like these...

And then had been thrust into one against her will.

God, please help her take a risk. Whatever You're asking her to do, help her to do it.

I think it's our only chance.

SEVENTEEN

Claire sat in the top of the lighthouse, door firmly locked with her inside, thankful that her hands were free. As long as she wasn't physically bound, she had hope. Maybe.

She walked to the window, wondering whether escape from it was possible, but one look down made her dizzy. No way was anyone escaping that way. Claire sat down, wanted to cry, but made herself go over her options.

Her eyes traveled back to the window. She really had only two choices. Take the risk and maybe die. Or stay in here… And almost definitely die.

She had to do this. And she *could* do this.

Claire repeated those words like a mantra as she took a deep breath and wedged herself carefully through the small window. It was just like rock climbing. Only with smaller, evenly shaped stones instead of rocks.

She was only about ten feet down when she heard familiar voices somewhere below her, inside the lighthouse—probably on the stairs. She recognized Brad's voice. The other was Nate. Her heart skipped and sunk. He'd come for her. She'd known he would, knew he cared enough to ignore any personal risk to try to save her. But she didn't need rescuing. And now he was in the hands of a drug smuggler and murderer.

Claire pushed off with one of her feet and continued free-climbing down the wall. The only way Nate was getting out of this alive was if Claire brought help. She wasn't stupid. She knew she couldn't take down Brad herself. But if she could get somewhere there was a cell signal, notify the police…

Cell phone. She squeezed her eyes shut, frustration making her head pound. Brad had taken hers, of course. Which meant her only choice was to get *all* the way to town, to the police station, and let them know about the situation in person. She could do it. She hoped.

As she continued her slow but steady descent, Claire's hands stung. She'd kept her skills up over the years, but mostly at rock gyms, designed for safety with chalk readily available. In fact, she hadn't done any real climbing since the accident that had caused Justin's death. But her muscles were well-toned. The motions were the same in a gym as they were in real life. If she could do it there, she could do it here.

Though the stakes were much, much higher.

And another man she loved might die if she made any mistakes.

Her breath quickened along with her heartbeat. The motions of climbing had been familiar in a good way until she'd had that thought about the accident. Now Justin's death was all she could think about. She remembered telling Justin that free-climbing Devil's Ledge, a sandstone structure in north Georgia, was foolish.

"It's sandstone, Justin. It crumbles in your hand." That was why Devil's Ledge was such a prize among the free-climbing community. Such an accomplishment.

Claire could count on one hand the people who had accomplished that feat.

"You said you wanted to take risks, Claire. Be more than a small-town girl who was born, grew up and died in the same place."

She'd laughed, tried to ease the tension, even as she internally flinched. Justin knew that that was a sore spot for her—that she worried that she wasn't exciting enough for him, and that that was why he had strayed. She'd felt the distance between them growing lately—not just physically, although their long-distance relationship had been the start of the trouble between them. *"Yeah, but I don't want to die here, either."* She'd meant it as a joke. Meant to convey how nervous the idea made her.

But not two hours later, the words would haunt her. For the rest of her life. Words that had come true, it seemed, though not for her…

She'd climbed with Justin anyway, so easily manipulated into taking his dare. She had been so determined to live life with no regrets over missed opportunities.

She wished someone had told her that it was possible to regret the opportunities she'd taken, too. Even now, almost a decade later, it was so easy to be right back there. And she was now. She took a deep breath, tried to ignore the echoing of Justin's screams in her ear as he'd slipped, lost one of his handholds.

She'd tried to save him…

But on that horrible day, there had been nothing she could do. By the time she'd climbed back down, losing her own handholds several times in the process, and even falling twelve feet onto a ledge and having to regroup and keep going, it had been too late for medical intervention to do any good.

Claire focused on the rock bricks of the lighthouse in front of her, hoping that effort would quell the dizziness. She struggled to keep her hands steady, keep her grip tight. This wasn't then. Justin was gone. She couldn't fix that now. But Nate was still here, still needed her.

God, help me do this. I know I can if You can steady my hands, help me focus, help me stop looking backward...just move one foot, one hand at a time...

Claire's mind couldn't seem to form any more words than that, but it was enough. She took a deep breath, felt a steadiness inside her, an echoing of firm reassurance. He would help. She could do this. She could.

Carefully she moved her feet along the stones of the lighthouse, feeling down with her toes to find the next spot where she could step down. Little by little she found new tiny outcroppings for her feet, then her hands, until finally, finally, she was nearing the bottom.

The bottom of the lighthouse, she remembered now, was made of smoother stones than the top. There were no outcroppings down there, no hand- or footholds. Her only choices were to jump and hope for the best—something that sounded more foolish than Claire liked—or climb back up and wait for death to come to her.

It was a risk. And sometimes risks weren't smart, like that climb at Devil's Ledge. But maybe...maybe not all risk was bad. Even though it had cost him his life, Claire knew Justin would have agreed. A life lived without any chances taken wasn't really lived at all. Sometimes, she realized as she hung on to the edges of the old lighthouse, you could train for risks, take them knowing you were capable of handling them. And sometimes you just had to take a leap of faith.

If she and Nate lived, if he still wanted to give whatever was between them a chance… Claire was ready to jump.

She swallowed hard, pushed off from the lighthouse and waited for the ground to connect with her feet. They hit solidly, and the impact brought her to her knees, but after a couple of seconds to catch her breath, she was fine. She'd done it.

Halfway there. Claire still needed to make it to town fast enough to get help for Nate. Otherwise…

No. She held on to the leap of faith she'd just taken, held on to the faith that had been growing in her heart. She wasn't even going to think about "otherwise."

She looked around, thankful that the area seemed to be clear. There were no signs that Brad was around or that he'd left his men nearby. They must still be inside with Nate. She had to hurry.

God, please help.

Claire ran as fast as she could until she reached Nate's motorcycle with the key waiting in the ignition. She could drive it or she could give up. And the second wasn't an option.

She turned the key, coaxed the clutch and the gas to cooperate enough to get forward motion. Gunned it down the road, lurching a little, but managing to keep her balance as her old skills slowly came back to her.

Claire couldn't believe she'd told Nate only days ago that she'd never get on this bike again. And now she was driving it.

If Claire had thought that riding on the back of a motorcycle was an adrenaline rush, driving one was even more so.

She pulled into the police department parking lot and

darted off the bike, then almost ran into the chief in the hallway.

"Claire. What are you doing here?"

"Nate Torres is being held in the old lighthouse by Brad Reid. Please send someone." She forced the words out around gasps for air. She'd barely gotten everything out by the time the chief was moving away from her, giving people instructions as he went.

"We'll get him," one of the officers who raced past assured her.

She nodded, hoping he was right, and ran back outside just in time to see four police cars race toward the lighthouse.

Claire hesitated as she watched them drive away. Nate would tell her to stay here, stay out of their way, not risk her life when there was a good chance there was nothing she could do...

Claire cranked the bike's engine back to life, made a somewhat wobbly turn, then hit the gas and burned up the road between town and the lighthouse.

She arrived just after the police cars and saw the officers circling the lighthouse.

"You stay back," the chief told Claire when he saw her. At least he knew better than to ask her to leave.

She obeyed but focused all her thoughts and prayers toward the lighthouse. Toward Nate. He had to be okay.

Everyone was staring at the lighthouse, and Claire could feel the buzz in the air, tension so thick it was almost tangible. No one seemed to know for sure if it was better to wait or to storm in.

Gunshots split the air, making their decision for them. It was time to act.

"Shots fired! Shots fired!"

"We're going in."

Claire had never prayed so hard in her life. She stared at the lighthouse, not sure what she would see, not sure if she should close her eyes like she did in scary movies.

But this wasn't a movie. This was her life.

Officers kicked down the front door, ran inside. She prayed for them, too. Waited long, agonizing minutes.

A lone figured jumped from one of the lower windows of the lighthouse, not ten feet off the ground.

"Jesse Carson! He's getting away!" Claire's scream got the attention of Clay Hitchcock, who took off running, catching up with the other man in very little time and pulling both his arms behind his back.

"We've got a body up here," an officer yelled from one of the windows.

Claire forgot to breathe.

"It's Brad Reid," the officer went on. "Nate Torres is up here, and he says that Jesse shot Reid. Nate's been shot, too—someone get an ambulance here."

Everything erupted into chaos then as Claire felt her head spin at the idea that Nate was hurt. He'd make it, right?

"Jesse Carson, you're under arrest," Claire heard Hitchcock say.

Claire's eyes swung back to the lighthouse. Waiting for Nate. How bad were his injuries? Could he walk?

And then, before she could wonder anymore, there he was, emerging from the lighthouse with the help of two police officers, one under each of his arms. The dark scarlet stain on his shoulder almost made her hurt there, too, she felt so deeply connected to him.

"You're not okay. I need you to be okay," she said

when Nate was close enough, not caring who was listening or watching, and certainly not caring what a crazy idea falling for Nate really was.

It was the best crazy idea she'd ever had.

"I'm going to be." Nate's warm gaze over her face was the closest they could get to an embrace right now.

Claire brushed a tear from her eye. This really was almost over. "You have to get to the hospital."

He nodded. "I'm not going to argue with you."

"What about me? Can I come?"

"There's no one I'd rather have with me."

"I'll get someone to drive me there."

The ambulance finally arrived, and they loaded Nate on a stretcher before roaring off. Claire wanted to get someone to take her there right away, but first she had to give her statement. And she needed a few minutes to just breathe in the air anyway, think about the fact that somehow she and Nate were still alive.

"I'll need to take you to the station, Claire," the chief told her. "Matt will take you home from there when you're done giving your statement…unless I'm right about the way you and that GBI agent looked at each other. In that case, he can take you to the hospital."

Claire smiled at the chief, then looked up at the sky as she walked back toward the chief's car.

Thanks for protecting us, God. Thanks for rock climbing, for making me brave enough to use it.

Claire looked back at the lighthouse one more time. Shook her head to dispel images of what might have been. And prayed for strength to put the entire thing behind her.

Because as the car drove away from the lighthouse,

Claire realized again, even more clearly than she had while climbing down the lighthouse, that she was ready to face the future, ready to take some risks and see what came next.

Nate didn't remember the rest of Christmas Eve past being loaded into the ambulance. Somehow knowing he was on his way to medical care told his body it would be okay to pass out. He'd done so and had been out most of the day as they worked on repairing the bullet's damage to his shoulder.

Though it had been a relatively clean wound according to the doctor, it was still a gunshot wound, so they weren't recommending he leave for another few days.

But it was Christmas. He knew Claire was planning to go to the Treasure Point Christmas carol sing at the town square that night—she'd left him a note last night when she'd been by that told him her plans and said she'd come to see him afterward—and he wanted to be at the carol sing, too.

"You know you should be in here for several more days." The doctor looked anything but happy with him when Nate announced his intention to sign himself out.

"I know. And I'm going to follow every one of your instructions to the letter," Nate assured him, holding up his discharge paperwork. "But it's Christmas. And there's this woman…"

The doctor still didn't look happy, but at least he nodded in understanding. "Call the number on that form if anything out of the ordinary happens. We can check you back in if we need to."

"Thank you."

Nate made his way to the front of the hospital, let

them wheel him outside as per hospital protocol and then climbed into the car that was waiting for him.

"You're sure about this?" Matt O'Dell asked. He motioned to Nate's shoulder. "That sounded like it was bad."

"It wasn't great, but they fixed it up. It'll be fine. Besides, it's not the first time I've been shot."

Matt didn't have any arguments to that, which Nate was thankful for. They drove in comfortable silence into Treasure Point, and Matt parked as close as he could to the square. "Claire and Gemma are on the right side, near the corner. I told Gemma to make sure Claire didn't run off anywhere."

"Thanks. I appreciate it."

Matt clapped a hand on Nate's good shoulder, although the impact still made Nate wince a little. "Welcome to the family," he said, then handed Nate the ring he'd picked up for him in Savannah. Nate had searched jewelry store's inventory from his phone in the hospital, and when he'd found the perfect one he'd bought it and asked Matt to pick it up for him.

"If she says yes," Nate reminded him.

Matt laughed. "I've seen the way she looks at you, man. She'll say yes."

Nate hoped he was right.

The Christmas tree in the middle of the square was lit up and beautiful. It was hard to believe that when the town had had the tree lighting ceremony, he and Claire hadn't been reunited yet. They'd fallen for each other fast, but their history made their relationship seem like it had lasted longer than a couple of weeks. Nate thought moving forward made sense.

Either that or he was crazy for asking her to marry

him so soon. But if this was crazy, that was fine with Nate. Being with Claire was worth it.

She didn't notice him approaching.

"Merry Christmas," he said when he'd come within a few feet of her.

Claire whirled around, eyes wide. "Nate! What are you doing here? I can't believe you're here."

"I didn't want to spend Christmas apart," he said, taking one of her hands. "Especially not what I hope will be our first Christmas out of a lot of them."

Her eyes widened, and Nate eased himself down onto one knee, careful not to use his right arm at all. With his left hand, he reached into the pocket of his jacket and pulled out a ring box. He opened it to reveal the ring he'd bought, a diamond surrounded by tiny sapphires—and Claire lifted a hand to her mouth.

"Claire Phillips, I love you. I want to spend the rest of our lives showing you how much, no matter where life takes us. Will you marry me?"

"Of course I will marry you, Nate Torres. You've turned my quiet life upside down, but I don't think I'd have it any other way."

He slid the ring onto her finger and then stood up next to her. He brushed a gentle kiss on her lips, thinking about how he'd never have guessed the last time they stood in this square that they'd be here just a week later—happy, in love and ready to start a future together.

They stood with the crowd for a little while longer, singing carols and celebrating Christmas. Nate loved hearing Claire sing. Her voice sounded just like her—sweet, clear and bold.

"I still can't believe you left the hospital and came

here. You could end up more badly injured," she whispered once between songs.

"I can believe it." He smiled at her and ran a hand down the side of her cheek before cupping it behind her head.

As he pulled her close, just before their lips met, he whispered, "Some risks are worth taking."

* * * * *

Don't miss these other exciting
TREASURE POINT *stories from Sarah Varland:*

TREASURE POINT SECRETS
COLD CASE WITNESS

Find more great reads at www.LoveInspired.com

Dear Reader,

People aren't always as they seem, are they? In Claire and Nate's story, I had such a fun time putting their characters together since they were very much opposites in how they appeared. Claire is always described as "sweet," and people don't see her as a risk taker or an adventurer, though deep inside she longs to be and *is* those things. And Nate is a rough-around-the-edges guy who rides a motorcycle and wears a lot of black, but there's plenty about his true character that doesn't fit any stereotype. In the end, they were both unique individuals—different than some people expected them to be, and they accept that about each other.

The person *you* are isn't a stereotype, either. God created you as a unique individual with a purpose, and it's my hope for you that you remember that. No matter what your day-to-day routine looks like, who you are can never been put into one box. We are too unique for that. Whatever your life looks like today and tomorrow, I hope that you will be open to God if He calls you to step out in a way you didn't expect. Following God can be unexpected, a life of adventure, but if we truly trust Him, He will lead us on the best path.

I love hearing from readers, and I'd love to hear from you! You can get in touch with me through email, sarahvarland@gmail.com, or find me on my personal blog, espressoinalatteworld.blogspot.com.

Sarah Varland

COMING NEXT MONTH FROM
Love Inspired® Suspense

Available December 6, 2016

ROOKIE K-9 UNIT CHRISTMAS
Rookie K-9 Unit • by Lenora Worth and Valerie Hansen
When danger strikes at Christmastime, two K-9 police officers meet their perfect matches in these exciting, brand-new novellas.

CLASSIFIED CHRISTMAS MISSION
Wrangler's Corner • by Lynette Eason
On the run to protect her late best friend's child, who may have witnessed his mother's murder, former spy Amber Starke returns to her hometown. But with the killer on her heels, she'll have to trust local deputy Lance Goode to help them survive.

CHRISTMAS CONSPIRACY
First Responders • by Susan Sleeman
When Rachael Long unmasks a would-be kidnapper after he breaks into her day care and tries to abduct a baby, she becomes his new target. But with first response squad commander Jake Marsh guarding her, she just might evade the killer's grasp.

STALKING SEASON
Smoky Mountain Secrets • by Sandra Robbins
Cheyenne Cassidy believes the stalker who killed her parents is dead—until he follows her into the Smoky Mountains and shatters her hopes of beginning a new life. Now Cheyenne must rely on Deputy Sheriff Luke Conrad to keep her safe from an obsessed murderer.

HAZARDOUS HOLIDAY
Men of Valor • by Liz Johnson
In order to help his cousin's struggling widow and her seriously ill son, navy SEAL Zach McCloud marries Kristi Tanner. And when he returns home from a mission to find that someone wants them dead, he'll do anything to save his temporary family.

MISTLETOE REUNION THREAT
Rangers Under Fire • by Virginia Vaughan
After assistant district attorney Ashlynn Morris's son goes missing, she turns to former army ranger Garrett Lewis—her ex-fiancé and the father of her child—for help finding him. But can Garrett keep Ashlynn alive long enough to rescue the son he never knew he had?

___

LOOK FOR THESE AND OTHER LOVE INSPIRED BOOKS WHEREVER BOOKS ARE SOLD, INCLUDING MOST BOOKSTORES, SUPERMARKETS, DISCOUNT STORES AND DRUGSTORES.

LISCNM1116

REQUEST YOUR FREE BOOKS!

2 FREE RIVETING INSPIRATIONAL NOVELS
PLUS 2 FREE MYSTERY GIFTS

Love Inspired®
SUSPENSE
RIVETING INSPIRATIONAL ROMANCE

YES! Please send me 2 FREE Love Inspired® Suspense novels and my 2 FREE mystery gifts (gifts are worth about $10). After receiving them, if I don't wish to receive any more books, I can return the shipping statement marked "cancel." If I don't cancel, I will receive 4 brand-new novels every month and be billed just $4.99 per book in the U.S. or $5.49 per book in Canada. That's a savings of at least 17% off the cover price. It's quite a bargain! Shipping and handling is just 50¢ per book in the U.S. and 75¢ per book in Canada.* I understand that accepting the 2 free books and gifts places me under no obligation to buy anything. I can always return a shipment and cancel at any time. Even if I never buy another book, the two free books and gifts are mine to keep forever.

123/323 IDN GH5Z

Name (PLEASE PRINT)

Address   Apt. #

City   State/Prov.   Zip/Postal Code

Signature (if under 18, a parent or guardian must sign)

Mail to the **Reader Service:**
IN U.S.A.: P.O. Box 1867, Buffalo, NY 14240-1867
IN CANADA: P.O. Box 609, Fort Erie, Ontario L2A 5X3

**Are you a current subscriber to Love Inspired® Suspense books
and want to receive the larger-print edition?
Call 1-800-873-8635 or visit www.ReaderService.com.**

* Terms and prices subject to change without notice. Prices do not include applicable taxes. Sales tax applicable in N.Y. Canadian residents will be charged applicable taxes. Offer not valid in Quebec. This offer is limited to one order per household. Not valid for current subscribers to Love Inspired Suspense books. All orders subject to credit approval. Credit or debit balances in a customer's account(s) may be offset by any other outstanding balance owed by or to the customer. Please allow 4 to 6 weeks for delivery. Offer available while quantities last.

Your Privacy—The Reader Service is committed to protecting your privacy. Our Privacy Policy is available online at www.ReaderService.com or upon request from the Reader Service.
We make a portion of our mailing list available to reputable third parties that offer products we believe may interest you. If you prefer that we not exchange your name with third parties, or if you wish to clarify or modify your communication preferences, please visit us at www.ReaderService.com/consumerchoice or write to us at Reader Service Preference Service, P.O. Box 9062, Buffalo, NY 14240-9062. Include your complete name and address.

LIS15

SPECIAL EXCERPT FROM

Love Inspired.
SUSPENSE

*When a CIA agent goes on the run home,
she'll need help from the local deputy to keep a
vulnerable young charge alive.*

Read on for a preview of
CLASSIFIED CHRISTMAS MISSION
by Lynette Eason, *the next exciting book in the*
WRANGLER'S CORNER series!

Deputy Lance Goode caught sight of headlights just ahead on the sharp curve and slowed. He focused on staying on his side of the road. The headlights came closer. Followed by a second set. Who was crazy enough to be out in this mess besides him?

He passed the first car and blinked. Even through the falling snow, he'd caught a glimpse of the driver. Amber Starke?

A loud crack split the quiet mountainside, and Lance stepped on the brakes. Chills swept over him. He'd heard that sound before. A gunshot.

When he looked back he saw Amber's SUV spin and then plunge over the side of the mountain. The vehicle behind her never stopped, just roared past.

Lance pulled to a stop. He headed to the edge to look over. He saw the tracks disappear under an overhang. Relief shot through him. Amber's sedan had only gone down the slight slope, under the overhang, and wedged

LISEXP1116

itself between two trees. Now he just had to find out if the bullet had done any bodily damage.

He ran to his SUV and opened the back. He grabbed the hundred-foot-length rope that he always carried with him and hefted it over his shoulder. He lugged it to the front of the Ford and tied one end to the grill then tossed the rest down to Amber's car. It reached, but barely. With one more glance over his shoulder, he grasped hold of the rope and slipped and slid down the embankment to the car. He was able to duck under the overhang and squeeze himself between the rock and the driver's door.

Amber lay against the wheel, eyes closed. Fear shot through. *Please let her be all right.* He reached for the door handle and pulled it open. It hit the rock, but there was enough room for her to get out if she wasn't too badly hurt.

Amber lifted her head and he found himself staring down the barrel of a gun.

Don't miss
CLASSIFIED CHRISTMAS MISSION
by Lynette Eason, available wherever
Love Inspired® Suspense books and ebooks are sold.

www.LoveInspired.com

LISEXP1116